AR: 9-12

KU-523-328

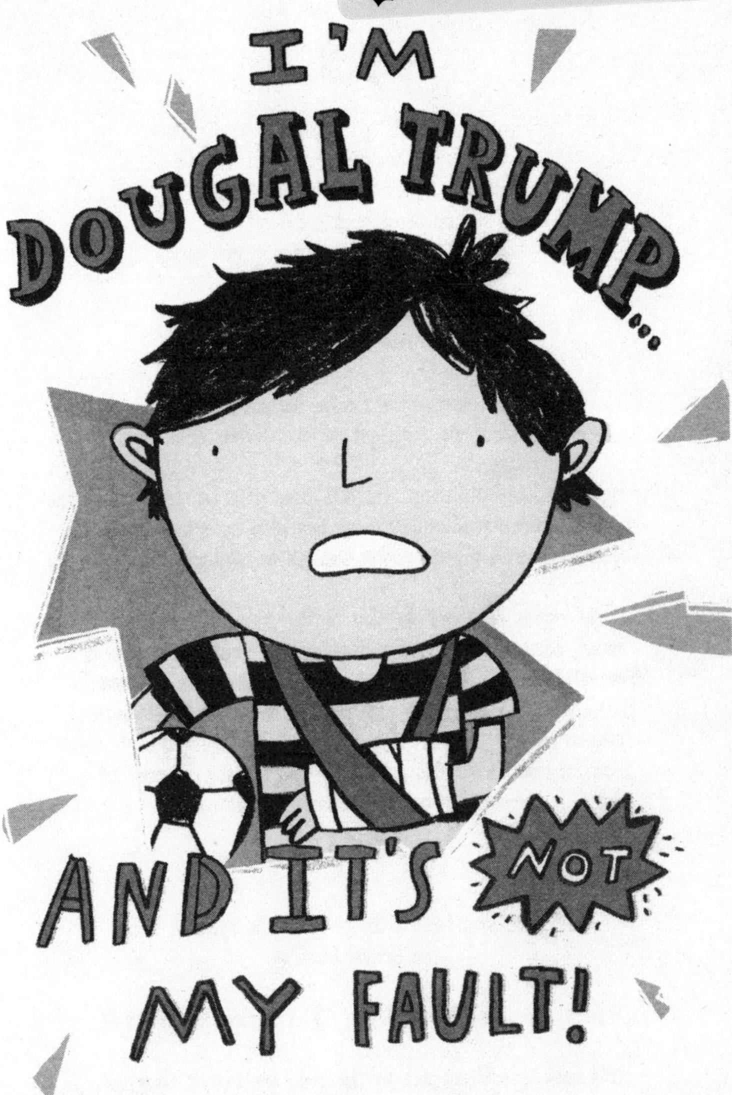

MACMILLAN CHILDREN'S BOOKS

First published 2012 by Macmillan Children's Books
a division of Macmillan Publishers Limited
20 New Wharf Road, London N1 9RR
Basingstoke and Oxford
Associated companies throughout the world
www.panmacmillan.com

ISBN 978-1-4472-1996-5

Text copyright © Jackie Marchant 2012
Illustrations copyright © Mike Lowery 2012

The right of Jackie Marchant and Mike Lowery to be identified as the author and illustrator of this work has been asserted by them in accordance with the Copyright, Designs and Patents Act 1988.

All rights reserved. No part of this publication may be reproduced, stored in or introduced into a retrieval system, or transmitted, in any form or by any means (electronic, mechanical, photocopying, recording or otherwise), without the prior written permission of the publisher. Any person who does any unauthorized act in relation to this publication may be liable to criminal prosecution and civil claims for damages.

1 3 5 7 9 8 6 4 2

A CIP catalogue record for this book is available from the British Library.

Printed and bound by CPI Group (UK) Ltd, Croydon CR0 4YY

This book is sold subject to the condition that it shall not, by way of trade or otherwise, be lent, resold, hired out, or otherwise circulated without the publisher's prior consent in any form of binding or cover other than that in which it is published and without a similar condition including this condition being imposed on the subsequent purchaser.

To all the kids who have to put up with families like mine.

To all the creatures who have to live in sheds like ours.

YOU LOOK GOOD ENOUGH TO EAT.

CONTENTS

I, DOUGAL TRUMP, AM DEAD.

OK, I'm not actually dead yet, but if I'm not very careful, I soon will be. And it's not just because my family and friends keep threatening to kill me.

I have absolutely no idea why my family and friends keep threatening to kill me. I am completely innocent of all the things they say I've done. It's not my fault they keep getting so annoyed they want to kill someone when I happen to be standing next to them.

As well as the above threats, I've had a note. I don't know who it's from, but they will kill me if I tell anyone what they've hidden in the shed.

This is the first time I've ever had a threat in writing, so I'm taking it very seriously.

Leabharlanna Poibli Chathair Baile Átha Cliath
Dublin City Public Libraries

It's the dog's fault.

And it's Mum's fault. She left a note as well, but it wasn't a threat to kill me.

at Gran's.

Back later.

Take dog out in Garden.

Mum's been spending a lot of time at Gran's, because Gran died a few weeks ago and left a load of stuff behind. She did leave a will, but it wasn't much help, as it just said everything must be split between Mum and my obscure aunt in Australia.

I have to admit that I didn't know what a will was before Gran died. Now I know it is simply a list of your possessions and who should have them when you die.

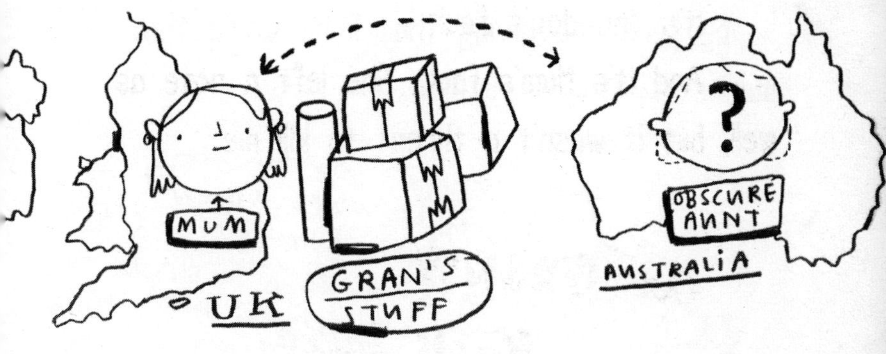

I'm beginning to think I need to write a will.

Mum says she doesn't know what to do with her half of Gran's stuff and there aren't enough charity shops in Ocklesford to put it all. Besides, she doesn't want to walk past a charity shop and see one of Gran's dresses on a model in the window. It will look like Gran's ghost has come back – but with a better figure.

Take dog out in garden. From the way the dog was looking up at me with his

soppy face and giving that little whine that means

I could tell Mum had been gone for a while.

Mum's note wasn't addressed to anyone, which meant that my big sister Sibble could have taken the dog out. But no amount of yelling upstairs was going to drag Sibble away from her life-or-death girlie activities. These include:

* Flicking her hair in front of the mirror.
* Putting nail varnish on.

* Taking nail varnish off.
* Gazing at her row of nail varnishes and wondering which one to choose.

* Gazing out of the window, wishing she was pretty enough to get a boyfriend.

* Threatening to kill her little brother because she's in a bad mood and he happens to be standing next to her.

By now the dog was looking like he was going to wet himself, so I let him out. He ran off, stopped, turned his head and gave me that look that says

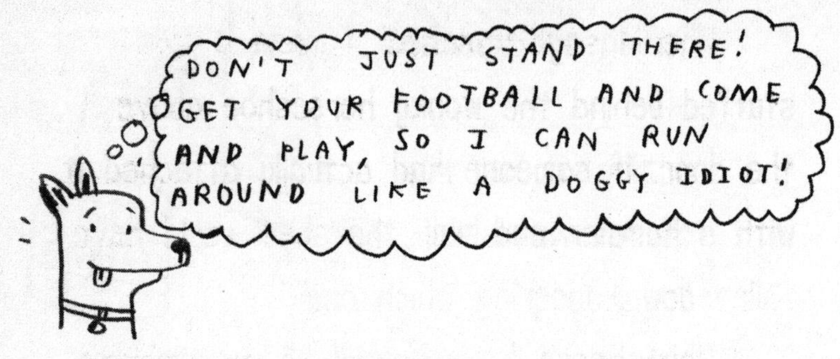

And that is why my life is now in great danger.

If the silly mutt hadn't run off with my football to the even wilder end of our garden, I'd never have found the note. It was attached to the shed.

When I say 'shed', that is how Dad describes the heap of wood at the bottom of our garden.

When I say 'attached', I mean it was stuffed behind the wonky horseshoe above the door. If someone had actually attached it, with a hammer and nail, the shed would have fallen down.

Which might have solved all my problems.

This is what the note said:

DO NOT DISTURB. CREATURE WILL BE COLLECTED IN THE NEXT 3 DAYS. TRANQUILLISERS WILL WEAR OFF SHORTLY. IF THE CREATURE WAKES, GIVE IT FRUIT AND KEEP IT QUIET, OR ELSE. IF IT DIES SO WILL YOU. IF ANYONE FINDS OUT WHAT IS IN THE SHED, YOU ARE DEAD.

NOW, EAT THIS NOTE.

The note didn't taste very nice. As I stood there chewing it, I noticed a scrabbling, snuffling and grunting sound – the stupid dog was trying to dig his way in. He must have a death wish.

The only way I could get him away was to give him the half-chewed note from my mouth, which he swallowed in one happy gulp. Then I grabbed his collar before he remembered the interesting smell in the shed. Unfortunately, as I bent down, my eye came close to a crack in the wood and I had a glimpse of what was in there.

I wish I hadn't.

There really is a creature in our shed. It's got teeth. Big ones. And claws. Even bigger.

I only hope it is collected before it wakes up. If not, it looks like it might spit out its fruit and eat me instead.

All things considered, I think it's time to make a will.

This is The LAST Will and TeSTAMENT of Me,

DOUGAL TRUMP,

OF 13 MAKEPEACE AVe, OCKLESFORD, MIDDLESEX.

I BEING OF SOUND MiND and BODY (FOR THE TIME BEING), MAKe This WiLL AS FollOWS:

My ashes must be scattered on the grounds of Stamford United Football Club at King's Road. NOWHERE ELSE! I would like my father, Raymond Trump, to scatter them. I must not be buried, because I don't want them to dig up their pitch for me.

My signed Stamford United goalkeeper's shirt must not be left to anyone. I will

wear it to the crematorium and it will be scattered on the ground at King's Road with the rest of me.

The cute little china dog Gran gave me when I was four years old and starting school should also go in the coffin with me. It should be hidden under my Stamford United goalie shirt so that no one can see it.

To my mother I leave all the mess on the floor in my room, which she may put into black bin-liners and throw out of the window. I know that has always been her greatest wish.

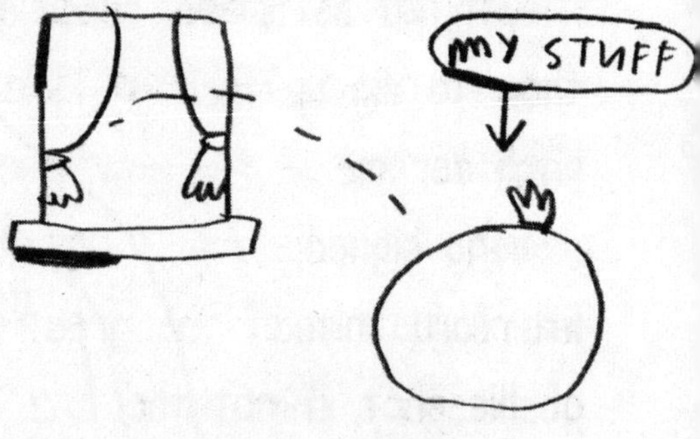

To my best friend, George Quickley, I leave my first plaster cast, which is now much too small for me, but might fit his skinny little arm. He might want to spray it with that stuff my mum uses to stop the smell. I leave this to him in memory of his cheating, that time we were having a race and I overtook him at the last minute to gain a spectacular victory. He tripped me up as I sped past him and I put my hand out to stop myself landing on my nose and breaking it. I broke my arm instead.

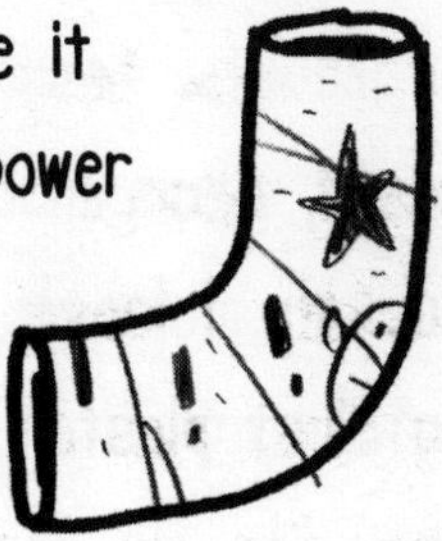

My second plaster cast I leave to my dad, to remind him that kicking a penalty as hard as you can at your son can and will damage his arm. And I suppose it will remind him of the great power of his shot, if not the accuracy, as the ball was supposed to go in the top corner. It will also remind him that his son made a spectacular save of his penalty.

My third plaster cast I leave to Uncle William, because he's a surgeon and showed some interest in my three broken arms (no, I haven't got three arms: I broke the right one twice).

I suppose I ought to leave something to my sister Sibble, who thinks she's it because she goes to Ocklesford High School, while I'm at Ocklesford Junior.

What could I leave that is suitable for a girl who tosses her hair all the time and never stops moaning because she can't find enough make-up to stop her from looking totally ugly?

Note to my Stupid brother, who is the only reason i ever moan: my Name is SYBIL! You can't spell and I'm not as ugly as you!!!

To SIBBLE I leave my scissors, so she can cut her hair off and stop flicking it in front of the mirror all the time.

My book of Stamford United autographs I leave to Mum, who took me to watch them train, even though she can't stand football and knows nothing about it. She got lost several times on the way and took me on a tour of big houses, which she thought was extremely interesting. The training session was over by the time we arrived. (I did manage

to get two autographs, from a changing-room attendant and a reserve in the B team. As far as I know, the B-team reserve has now left the club for a career as a deputy assistant manager at a very well-known fast-food joint.)

To the dog I leave all my odd socks so he can eat them as well as their partners, which he has eaten already. Swallowing socks is very dangerous for a dog, because sometimes they have to go to the vet and have a big operation to remove the sock and the dog might even die. But our dog seems to swallow socks quite happily and then wait for them to come out of one end or the other. (Note: he doesn't eat them again if they come out of the other end.)

If Mum gets cross because the dog has eaten one of my socks, I always remind her of the time we had to stop on a zebra crossing because the dog wanted to do a poo. All the cars stopped and everyone watched as something very long and stretchy came out of the dog. Mum had to keep pulling it out, with her hand wrapped in a plastic bag. She went very red when she realized it was a pair of her own tights. I told her that she shouldn't leave her tights lying around for the dog to eat. She told me to shut up because everyone could hear what I said and the people in their cars had stopped being cross and were now laughing and pointing.

Dougie, please could you spend less time on your will and more time tidying your room? I think it would be nice if I could see some of your floor.

Love, MUM

P.S. Have you done your homework?

To my mum I leave my toy telescope, so she can see that there are lots of bits of floor to be seen in my room. I have counted at least three.

To my teacher, Mr Truss, I leave any homework that Mum finds in my room, together with a note to say that she's sorry it's late.

The carrier bag of pictures, poems and other work I have done at school, which Mum has kept, should be divided equally between

Mum and Ocklesford Junior School. My best work should be displayed clearly around the house. The ace drawing of me scoring a hat-trick at King's Road in a Stamford United 7, Arsenal 0 game should be put up in the school office.

The school can also have the clay model of a dog I made in Year Three. It's lost its head and tail, but still looks like a dog. In fact, it looks more like a dog now than it did before its head and tail fell off. That happened when Sibble threw it at me because I said she had hairy legs. I think it looks rather like our own dog, who is of indeterminate breed.

Reminder to my STUPID brother: I do NOT have hairy legs! AND your drawings are RUBBISH!

I leave all my books to the school library, with the following inscription inside each one: *Left to Ocklesford Junior School by their star pupil, Dougal Trump. He will be sadly missed – he couldn't have tried harder even if he tried. He was our most trying pupil.*

All my football clothes should be given to Mr Goff the sports teacher, so he can add them to the pile he is sending to Africa. There should be enough for a five-a-side Stamford United team in full kit of various sizes.

The contents of my dressing-up box I leave to Mrs Minns for the school plays – she should be very careful with the sword though, as the man at the jumble sale said it's a real one and could do some damage, even though it is a bit blunt.

Dad can also have my football boots. If

he hadn't become a window cleaner, he says he might well have been a professional footballer. Mum says it's lucky he chose windows.

I DON'T WANT YOUR BOOTS. THEY STINK AND ARE COVERED IN MUD BECAUSE YOU NEVER CLEAN THEM.

– DAD

PS – STOP ANNOYING YOUR SISTER.

The posh statue of a footballer, which Uncle William gave me, I give to Tom, the coach of my team, Ocklesford Rovers. Tom can use it as the Man of the Match trophy. It will replace the one that got kicked into the river by mistake when I was showing Claude Barleycorn how to do a goal-kick. I leave all my old footballs to my next-door neighbour, Mrs Grim, so she can keep them in her garden and never give them back to me (no change there then).

To the neighbours on the other side I can't leave anything because they've moved. When I asked them where they were moving to, they said as far away as possible. When I asked them why they were moving, they muttered something about noisy dogs and footballs.

COOL WILL, DOUGIE! THANKS FOR THE CAST. CAN I HAVE YOUR PLAYSTATION TOO?

– GEORGE

To my best friend, football ace George Quickley, I leave my PlayStation – and all its games, as long as he admits that I am the best goalie ever.

Note to my STUPID brother: that PlayStation is HALF MINE! It was a joint Christmas present, remember? So you can't leave it to anyone without my permission.

My PlayStation must be cut in half. Half of it will go to George and the other half to Sibble, who never plays with it. ALL my PlayStation games will go to George.

My collection of football programmes I leave to Claude Barleycorn because he's an Arsenal supporter and it will drive him mad to have a load of Stamford United programmes

that he is not allowed to destroy because I said so in my will.

To my hamster I leave all the bits of dried food that have made their way right under my bed. At the last count I had a couple of wizened apple cores (these are very old – it's a long time since I ate an apple), frizzled orange peel (twelve small pieces. I don't eat oranges any more either – I gave

them up at the same time as apples), raisins (several), fragments of crisps (I lost count after eighty-six), peanuts (two) and an old piece of chocolate, which was covered in spider web.

The fluffy mouse, which I got to scare Mrs Grim with, I leave to the cat.

To my mum I leave the fifteen black bin-liners full of Gran's stuff, which she has dumped in my room 'just for a little while' (which means a very big while). Mum put these bin-liners in my room because she isn't ready to chuck all that stuff out yet. Besides, some of it is too embarrassing to give away.

In one of the bags I found some huge knickers and I would like to leave these to Mrs Minns. They should be big enough to

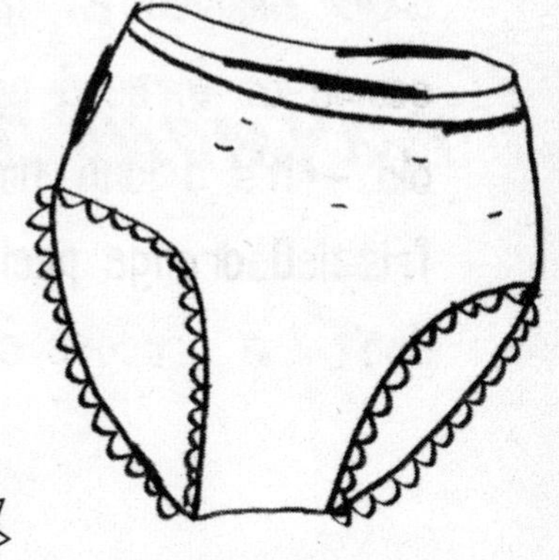

fit her large bottom, which she ought to know looks terribly wobbly when she cycles to school.

My daily share of the brown goo that Mum cooks for us I leave to the dog, as he seems to like it.

This is my last will and testament, signed by me:

Dougal TRUMP

in the presence of witnesses:

CHRISTABEL TRUMP

Mum

RAYMOND TRUMP

Dad

I am not signing this stupid will - I hate you.

~~Sibble~~

It's SYBIL, you dork.

I, DOUGAL TRUMP, AM EVEN DEADER THAN BEFORE.

That is to say I am still alive, but only just.

The creature in the shed has woken up.

I came home from school to find a big lorry outside the neighbours' house and a man directing an enormous cream sofa in through the front door. Mum says cream is not very practical if you have a dog like us (I don't think anyone has a dog like us – ours is unique).

I went up to my room, changed into my Stamford United shirt, looked out of my window and saw the same man come into the back garden. He put a couple of boxes down in the gap between our houses, where Dad keeps his ladders. He then took a good look

over the fence at our garden. I was sure he was looking right at the shed. I dashed outside, remembering the note – especially the bit about being dead if anyone found out what was in there.

'Hello,' I said.

'Oh, hello, mate,' he said, in that voice Dad uses when he doesn't want me to disturb him.

'Our dog sometimes gets through here.' I nodded at the hole in the fence. 'Dad's been meaning to fix it.'

'What type of dog have you got?'

'The mutt type.'

'Oh. What's his name?'

'The Dog.'

'Yes, what's his name?'

'The Dog,' I repeated.

He didn't look very impressed.

'That's short for his full name,' I said. 'Which is Oi, You, The Dog!'

He looked even less impressed.

'My sister wanted to call him Doggy-pops,' I continued. This was great. He hadn't looked at the shed once while we were talking. 'We've got a cat as well,' I offered.

'Let me guess,' he said. 'It goes by the name of The Cat?'

I nodded. 'My sister wanted to call him Fluffy-wuffy Puss-kins.'

'Ri-ight,' he said. The man looked like he was getting fed up with this line of conversation, so I changed tack.

'What's in the boxes?' I asked, imagining The Dog sinking his teeth into the cardboard and eating whatever was inside.

'Never you mind. They'll be gone soon. Nice garden, by the way.'

'We've got a wild bit by the house,' I explained. 'Then a wilder bit in the middle and an even wilder bit at the end, where the shed is.'

'Shed?'

I could have kicked myself. Instead, I stood there imagining our new neighbour telling everyone what was in the shed. Or being eaten by the creature. I had to think quickly. 'It's falling to bits and we don't use it,' I said.

'Could I have a look?' he asked.

'Honestly, it's a health hazard,' I said. 'It might fall down on your head.'

I'D STAY AWAY
IF I WERE YOU...

He laughed. 'What's your name, mate?'

'Dougie. What's yours?'

'You can call me Mr Witzel. So, you support Stamford United?'

I nodded.

'So does my son, Stan,' said Mr Witzel, lifting his head up over the fence again. 'Now, why don't you show me this shed of yours?'

'There's nothing to see, Mr Witzel,' I said. 'There is absolutely nothing in it.'

'Empty, is it? I wonder if I could store some of my boxes there then.'

'No! You don't want to do that. It leaks.'

'I could fix it for you.'

'No thanks, Mr Witzel. I quite like it leaking.'

'Why?'

I had to do more quick thinking. 'It's my den. A secret den. The leaking stops other people going in.'

'I see.' He winked at me. 'I used to have a secret den. I wonder if it was like yours. What do you keep in there?'

'I told you. Nothing. Nothing at all. I haven't been near it for ages because I'm too old for dens now.'

'So there *is* space for some boxes?'

I was beginning to panic. 'Where's your son?' I asked, to change the subject.

'Stan? His mum's bringing him over. They'll be here any minute. I'm sure he'd love a look in your den.'

Again I had to think fast. 'Uh . . . I'd better go in, Mum will be home from work soon.'

I dashed indoors, ran upstairs and looked out of my window. Mr Witzel was examining the plank that is supposed to stop the dog going through the gap in the fence. The next thing I knew, he had moved the plank, climbed into our garden and started scrambling through the brambles to the shed.

I have never run so fast. I tore through the brambles and nettles in the even wilder bit, destroying my school trousers. 'I told you,' I panted. 'That shed is secret and only I am allowed in there.' And to prove my point, I pulled the door open, stepped in and closed it behind me.

I sat there in the dark.

Now I know why people wet themselves when they are scared.

The smell was like our dog, but ten times worse. The noise was like the dog's heavy breathing, but ten times louder. At first I could only see a large lump in the gloom, but then my eyes adjusted and I could see long, shiny black fur. And claws, even bigger than I remembered.

The creature snorted in its sleep and shuffled.

When I say 'snorted', it was more of a deep, menacing growl.

At the same time, there was a bang on the door and the whole shed rattled. 'You all right in there?' shouted Mr Witzel.

That was when the creature woke up.

A very large head popped up to see what all the noise was about. I only had time to see two glinting eyes looking at me, then I was outside the shed, with my back to the door, legs crossed because I was trying very hard not to wet myself. 'Fine,' I squeaked, giving Mr Witzel my best smile.

Mr Witzel looked behind me. His eyes widened. 'What on earth is *that*?'

I didn't want to look. I heard snarling and movement in the undergrowth as I saw Mr Witzel run to the gap in the hedge. The creature must have escaped and now I was dead. Then I felt something squirming against my leg.

I looked down and laughed with relief. It was only our mad dog. I managed to grab his collar and haul him through the wilder bit into the wild bit, where I found Mum at the back door.

'Who were you talking to in the garden?' she asked.

'He's our new next-door neighbour, Mr Witzel,' I said. 'His son supports Stamford United.'

'That's nice,' said Mum.

I didn't tell her I was about to die.

Note to whoever left the creature in the shed:

I'd be very grateful if you could take it away **as soon as possible**. It's been in there for nearly a week now and it's very much awake. I don't know if I can find enough fruit for it. I don't know how much longer I can keep it a secret, as it's very noisy at night. I've been practising grunting so everyone thinks the noises are coming from me, but I don't know how long I can keep this up.

ALSO, I really don't want to be murdered by an unknown method if anything happens to the creature. Enough people I know want to **KILL** me, without this additional threat.

Tomorrow would be a good time to collect it, while I'm at school and my parents are at work. Be careful of Mr Witzel, he can be a bit nosy.

Yours Anxiously,

Dougal Trump

PS - If the wrong person finds this note, please don't tell anyone or I will be **dead**.

PPS - I'll eat this note, just to be safe.

PPPS - Second thoughts, I'll feed it to the dog - he'll eat anything.

I, DOUGAL TRUMP, would
Like TO MAKE it KNOWN
that SOMEONE WANTS
to KILL ME.

If I am found dead, please give this message to the police immediately, so they can arrest the person responsible.

In order to help the police with their enquiries, I list below the people who have threatened to kill me and their preferred methods, so that the appropriate murderer can be brought to justice.

My sister Sibble:

She has threatened to do the following:

Bury me alive. If this is the case, please dig me up and cremate me so that my ashes can be scattered at the grounds of Stamford United. Before doing this, please

make sure that I really am dead. Leave the coffin lid open so that if Sibble hasn't managed to kill me properly, I can sit up like a vampire in a horror film and give everyone a scare.

Cremate me alive. If this is the case, please torture Sibble (Chinese burns make her scream and she goes berserk if you put a spider on her bare leg) until she reveals the location of my ashes.

Force me to eat poison. She needn't bother, as I think Mum is already trying this with her cooking.

I would suggest that Sibble is the prime suspect because she has come up with the most methods of murdering me.

Note to my stupid, but unfortunately not dead yet, brother: here are a couple of extra suggestions, in case the others don't work. <u>Throw you to the wolves</u> (though the poor things might get sick after eating you). <u>Chuck you in a pit of poisonous snakes</u>, and watch you writhe and squirm until you can writhe and squirm no more.

Love and kisses, SYBIL

I would like the police to take note of the above further threats from Sibble.

Mum:

If I am found starved to death in my room, that would have been Mum. She is always threatening to lock me in my room until it is tidy.

Dad:

If I have been strangled with the PlayStation cord, that would have been Dad, because I beat his high score again.

Claude Barleycorn:

If I have been bludgeoned to death with a banana, that would have been Claude. I don't think Claude will be a suspect.

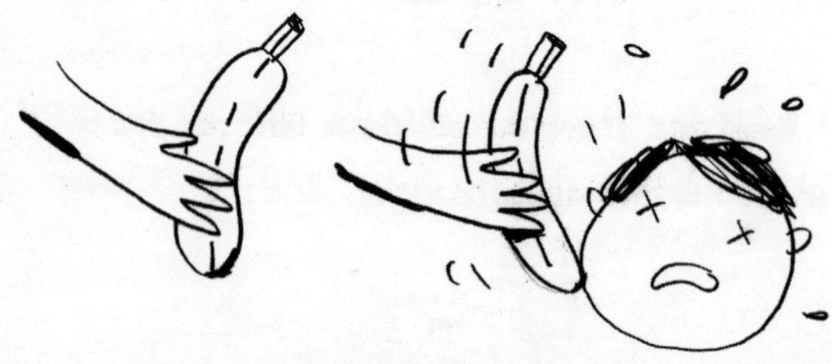

Angela Sweeter:
If I have stuck my own head down the toilet and flushed it until I drowned, that would have been because Angela told me to when I tried to kiss her.*

The creature in the shed:
If I have disappeared without a trace, I have been eaten by the creature in the shed.

If I have been murdered in any way other than the above, it would have been the person who left the creature in the shed. He or she didn't specify a method.

* Please note – I only did this because Sibble said that no girl would ever let me kiss her, ever.

AMENDMENTS to the Last Will and Testament of DOUGAL TRUMP

I, Dougal Trump, would like to LEAVE the FOLLOWING items to the FOLLOWING people:

- THE cat – Nothing
- THE HAMster – NothiNG
- MUM – NothiNG
- THE DOG – NothiNG
- SiBBLE – ABSOLUTELY NOthiNG EVER AGAiN
- MRS GRIM – LESS thAN NothiNG
- DAD – EVEN LESS than NothiNG
- UNCLE WilliAM – I SHOULD HAVE NEVER LEFT HIM ANY thiNG IN tHE FiRST PLACE

The above are all disinherited. That means they are out of my will and they get nothing. This is why.

The cat:
For starting it all, by sitting on the kitchen counter and staring at the dog until he freaked out and started barking, which drove Mum mad. I was outside at the time, kicking the ball against the fence, to disguise the banging noises coming from the shed.

The creature still hasn't been collected, you see. I've been collecting as much fruit as I can and hiding it until I can sneak out and stuff it through a hole in the shed. I've found a brilliant hiding place for my fruit – inside my collection of plaster casts.

Mum:
For making me clean the hamster's cage, and blaming me when the hamster escaped.

The hamster:
For escaping from his cage. The cat tried to catch the hamster and the dog tried to catch them both. Mum made me come in from the garden and catch the hamster. Then I had to take the dog out in the garden, as she was threatening to kill us both. When I asked her, just out of curiosity, what murder method she was going to use, she got even crosser.

The dog:
For biting my ankles while I was trying to make a spectacular save of my own shot at goal. While I was rubbing my ankles better, he ran off with the ball.

I wrestled the ball back off him and had my revenge by using him as target practice. But he jumped up and nosed the ball like a seal into Mrs Grim's garden – right through the window of her new greenhouse.

Sibble:
For chasing me along Mrs Grim's wall because I was running away with her knickers. It's not my fault that Sibble's knickers were the only white things available on the washing line to use as a white flag of surrender to wave at Mrs Grim in apology.

It's not my fault Sibble fell off the wall and broke her leg.

Mrs Grim:
For taking no notice of my white knickers of peace when she came storming out of her house to shout at me about the greenhouse.

Dad:
For making me apologize to Mrs Grim for breaking her greenhouse and waving knickers at her. Then for making me clear up the mess in her compost bin, which had nothing to do with me.

I was just putting the lid back on when I noticed a jagged hole at the back of our shed. Stuck to the jagged hole I could see several thick, long, wiry black hairs. There were bits of rotting wood on the ground as

well. It looks like something has burst out of our shed.

I think I know what burst out of our shed.

I know what made the mess in Mrs Grim's compost bin.

Then a black face and pair of wild eyes appeared at the hole. The creature must have decided to go back to the shed after trashing Mrs Grim's garden, thank goodness.

Dad (again. He is even more out of my will than everyone else):
For making me clean the car for free, to cover the cost of a new pane of glass for Mrs Grim's greenhouse. And I have to do Sibble's paper round and give her all the money from it.

Worst of all, Dad made me apologize to Sibble, even though it wasn't my fault she decided to fall off a wall and break her leg. Mum said I would jolly well have to push Sibble around in her wheelchair. I was quite looking forward to that, but Sibble wouldn't let me near her.

Then, after all that, Dad grounded me for the WHOLE WEEKEND!

While I was grounded, Mum made me tidy up my room. She stood in the middle (after she'd cleared a space for her feet), pointing at

things and telling me to pick them up. Luckily Mum didn't find the casts full of fruit that I've hidden under the bed, although she did keep sniffing and asking what the funny smell was.

One thing I did find was the key to the shed. It was tucked behind my bucket of old conkers, which I collected when I was about five. Now they've gone mouldy and Mum wants me to throw them out. I refused, as they had actually gone a really interesting turquoise colour.

While we were arguing, I managed to sneak the shed key into my trouser pocket. I thought that locking the shed would stop anyone from going in there, thereby improving my chances of not being killed by an unspecified method. And the creature can come and go as it pleases through the hole in the back of the shed.

Uncle William:
For scaring Mum by telling her all the awful things that could happen to Sibble's broken leg. If Sibble ends up with a funny-shaped leg it might make her more interesting. She might end up walking around in circles.

Note to my stupid brother: For your information, I have decided to write my own will. <u>In which I am leaving you nothing</u>.

All the possessions that I was going to leave to the disinherited I now leave to George and Claude. To George because he swore on his pet worm Harold's life not to tell anyone about the creature in the shed and for promising to find bits of fruit for it. To Claude for swearing on his cuddly hamster's life (his mother won't let him have a real one) that he wouldn't breathe a word about the creature. He's given me a large jar of marmalade for it. That's because he had a peek through a hole in the shed and has decided that I've got Paddington Bear in there.

If I remember correctly from my childhood days, Paddington was rather smaller than that.

DEAR DOUGIE,

i'm stan witzel and you Live Next door to ME NOW. Your MUM SAYS you are grounded, so here is a Note. MEET me by the gap in the hedge Near the bottom of the garden as soon as you can sneak out.

- STAN

DOUGIE,

I CAME ROUND TODAY TO PLAY ANOTHER GAME OF SWORD-FIGHTING WITH CRUTCHES, BUT YOUR SISTER SAID YOU WERE GROUNDED AND YOUR MUM SHOULDN'T HAVE LET ME IN YESTERDAY EITHER.

SEE YOU IN SCHOOL TOMORROW (MONDAY).

– GEORGE

Note to my STUPID, annoying and deaf brother: LEAVE MY CRUTCHES ALONE!!! I Need them and don't want to search your stinking room for them every time you take them. They are NOT toys!!! If you dare touch them again, I will Bang you over the head with one of them and wrap the other one around your stupid Neck.

Note to the police:

IF I have BEEN KiLLED BY A pAiR OF CRUTCHES, that WOULD HAVE BEEN SiBBLE.

DEATH BY CRUTCHES

Hi DOUGiE,

STAN HERE. I ASKED MY DAD iF HE COULD GET ME into YOUR OCKLESFORD ROVERS TEAM AND he said HE should bE ABLE to FiX that FOR ME.

Why DiD you KEEP Looking behind you whilE WE were AT THE HEDGE?

Dear Dougie,

George said you were grounded so i am going to sneak down the alley at the back of the houses to feed ~~Paddington bear~~ the creature in the shed.

from Claude

(PS) i hope no one one finds out about the creature because I don't want you to be **DEAD**.

DOUGIE, it's me, Stan.

I WANT to FORMALIZE IN WRiting what we agreed when we met at the gap in the hedge - if I help with your sister's paper round, I want half the money.

BY the way, my dad said you had a den in your shed. Next time, Let's meet in there.

Dear Dougie,
I think I might have
got the wrong
shed.

– Claude

I think there's something
in your shed.

– Stan

DOUGIE,
I SAW A STRANGE BOY IN
YOUR GARDEN LOOKING AT YOUR
SHED. HE DOESN'T LOOK VERY
NICE. THOUGHT I'D BETTER
WARN YOU, HOPE YOU GET THIS
NOTE.

– GEORGE

sorry you've BEEN grounded for even longer Because you came round to my house. Thanks for telling me what is in the shed. Don't worry, I didn't tell anyone. I'm your friend - you CAN TRUST me! ☺

- STAN

NOTE TO my STUPID Brother: STOP making SILLY noISES in your SLeep.

From your sensible sister, SYBIL.

PS. Dad says I can have a Rabbit for my birthday, SO there.

DEAR DOUGIE,

WHY WEREN'T YOU IN SCHOOL TODAY? WHAT HAS HAPPENED? DON'T WORRY, CLAUDE AND I WILL STILL FEED THE CREATURE. CLAUDE KNOWS WHICH SHED IT IS NOW.

THERE ARE TWO NEW BOYS IN OUR CLASS. ONE IS CALLED BILLY AND HE IS OK, BUT THE OTHER ONE IS THAT BOY I SAW NEAR YOUR SHED.

I <u>STILL</u> <u>DON'T</u> <u>LIKE</u> <u>HIM</u>.

I'VE TOLD THE GIRLS THAT YOU ARE VERY ILL IN HOSPITAL AND WILL DIE IF YOU DON'T GET LOTS OF FRUIT. THEY BELIEVED ME AND GAVE ME FRUIT FROM THEIR LUNCH BOXES.

SEE YA,

GEORGE

i think i've got the right shed now. there was definitely something in the one I left the fruit in. It's Got big CLAWS.

From, Claude

DEAR DOUgie,

HERE is SOME FRUIT. GEORGE SAYS YOU are IN HOSPITAL BUT WE DON'T BELIEVE HIM. BUT → YOU CAN HAVE OUR FRUIT ANYWAY.

–ANGELA SWEETER

xxx

I, DOUGAL TRUMP, VERY NEARLY DIED. FROM EMBARRASSMENT.

It's Mrs Witzel's fault.

She really ought to know better than to lean over the fence to stroke the dog while she is hanging up her washing. Especially when she is holding a bra.

The bra dangled over the fence just as the dog jumped up. I did try to tell Stan's mum to be careful, because our dog will eat anything, but I didn't want to yell the word 'bra' too loudly. Then it was too late.

'Don't worry, I'll get it back!' I promised Mrs Witzel, as I ran after the dog.

Luckily I managed to get hold of the strap when it got caught on a bramble in the wilder bit. Unluckily the dog thought we were having a game of tug-of-war. After a lot of

pulling and tugging, we ended up by the shed.

I had the strap in two hands and leaned back with all of my weight, but the dog still wouldn't let go. Then the bra ripped in half.

I went crashing back into the shed. I was sure that I'd wake the creature up, but it didn't make a sound. I think it might have been out. Or dead.

I do hope my creature isn't dead.

I went back to Mrs Witzel, who was watching from the fence. By that time, the dog had swallowed his half of the bra.

'Don't worry,' I said, giving her the other half. 'I'll bring the rest of it back when the dog sicks it up.'

Mrs Witzel didn't say anything. She just walked back to her house with half a bra drooping from her fingertips, leaving the rest of her washing in the basket. I was going to call after her to tell her she'd forgotten to hang it up, but Sibble came hobbling out of the house to remind me in a very loud, squeaky, girlie voice that I shouldn't have been out because I am grounded. I am only allowed out to do her paper round.

I didn't get very far with Sibble's paper round. It's Mrs Grim's fault. And the *Ocklesford Gazette*'s fault.

the OCKLESFORD GAZETTE
MAKEPEACE AVENUE BINS TRASHED

It was all about how something's been going down the bins in our road at night, strewing rubbish everywhere and leaving a terrible mess. Urban foxes have been blamed. We are now advised not to leave our bins out at night. Instead we have to rise before dawn to put them out before the bin-men come round. We are also advised not to leave fruit in our compost bins as urban foxes seem to have suddenly developed a liking for fruit. And vegetables.

You'd think they'd have something better to write about. You'd think they'd know the difference between carnivorous urban foxes and large creatures who live in sheds and like hunting for fruit at night. I hope the creature's getting enough to eat – I don't want him getting hungry.

Anyway, I had my nose stuck in the

paper, and that's when my foot caught Mrs Grim's silly one-brick-high wall and I went flying, along with all the newspapers. I crashed to the ground, stuck my arm out to save myself . . . and now it's broken.

As well as complaining to the council about the bins, I also heard Mrs Grim telling Mum that she thinks we should have wheelie bins instead of having to put our rubbish out like the third world. Then she told Mum she was sure she saw someone in her garden the other night.

It wasn't a some*one* she saw, it was a some*thing*. I saw it too.

I'm seriously thinking I might have to start sleepwalking as well as making funny noises at night.

I'm also seriously thinking that I must have a very interesting medical condition

that means my bones keep breaking. I think Mum was worried about this as well, because I heard her on the phone to Uncle William about it. He talks so loudly that Mum has to hold the phone away from her ear, so you can hear everything. This was his verdict on my interesting bone condition:

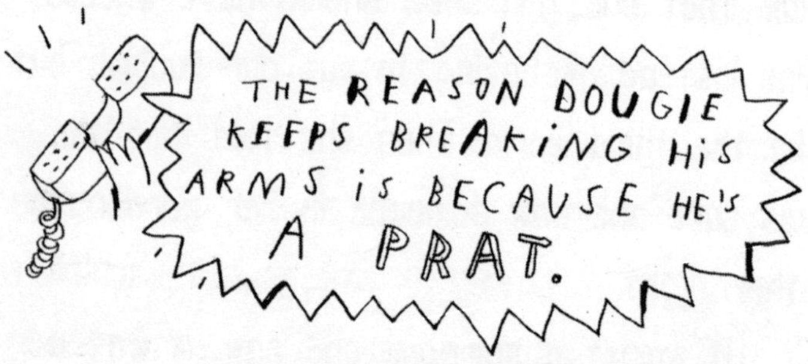

THE REASON DOUGIE KEEPS BREAKING HIS ARMS IS BECAUSE HE'S A PRAT.

I've decided that, if I ever write another will, Uncle William won't be in it.

That is the reason I wasn't back in school on Monday. I was in hospital chatting to the nurses who remembered me from last time. And the time before.

One even remembered the first time. She says I've grown a bit since then, but I'm obviously still as careless.

When we got home from hospital, we found the dog quivering and moaning in his bed. We had to rush him straight to the vet's, where he had a life-or-death operation to remove half of Mrs Witzel's bra.

As well as half a bra, the vet also found a small rubber ball (I remember the dog swallowing that some time ago), several paper clips, a bottle of Sibble's nail varnish (I told her I hadn't stolen it!), a small rubber duck (must have been in there for ages), a toy soldier, two socks (not matching) and two scrunched-up pieces of paper. Luckily the vet didn't open them up and read them – they were the notes about the creature that I'd got the dog to swallow. I told Mum they were the pieces of homework he'd eaten when she wouldn't believe me.

While Mum was paying the vet's bill (a very large one), I managed to corner the vet and ask him what sort of creature is big and furry, with large claws, sharp teeth and makes funny noises at night. He said there was no such thing. Not in Ocklesford, anyway.

My creature is unique!

The dog survived his operation and is now looking very sorry for himself with a big bandage round his tummy and one of those silly lampshade collars to stop him from licking his wound.

I was hoping the vet would find the TV remote, but he didn't, so Dad will still carry on blaming me for losing it.

Despite my promise to Mrs Witzel, I couldn't give the half a bra back to her because the vet threw it away. Mum said Mrs Witzel probably wouldn't mind. Sibble said I was disgusting and gross.

DEAR DOUgiE,
I'M GOING to write a
WiLL Like YOU DiD. WOULD
YOU Like my fLUffy TOY
HAMSTer? I CAN't HAVE A
REAL ONE BECAUSE MUM
Doesn't Like them. IF
YOU WANT it, I COULD Bring
it rOUNd sometime.

from CLAUDe

I, DOUGAL TRUMP, AM IN A DILEMMA.

A DILEMMA IS WHAT HAPPENS WHEN YOU ARE TORN IN TWO. I DON'T MEAN REALLY BEING TORN IN TWO, ALTHOUGH THAT MIGHT STILL HAPPEN IF THE CREATURE HAS HIS WAY.

I'm torn in two because of George, Billy Something-or-Other and Stan.

Maybe that means I'm in a trilemma – torn in three.

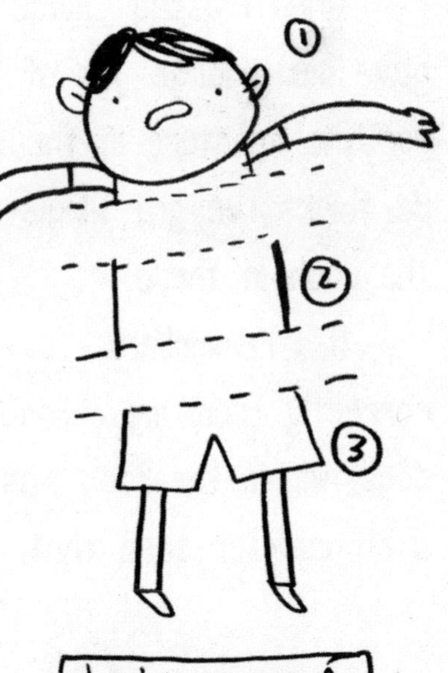

It's Billy Something-or-Other's fault.

For some reason, George has decided he doesn't trust Stan. He is furious with me for telling Stan about the creature, so to pay me back he told Billy Something-or-Other about the creature too.

How could he do that, when we've only known Billy for five minutes? AND Billy plays in goal for Fairford United, the worst team in our league.

When I asked Claude to back me up, he gave me a large jar of honey for the creature in the shed. He thinks I've got Winnie-the-Pooh in there.

If I remember correctly from my childhood days, Winnie-the-Pooh was a bit cuddlier than that.

Then I got told off by our teacher Mr Truss for talking. Just me. Not the others.

Then, while everyone went to after-school football training, I had to walk home with Sibble and her girlie friend.

Sibble made me walk four paces behind them. I walked along, arm in a sling, kicking the ground, wishing I could be at football training. Stan would be there and so would George and Billy. Stan told me that his dad has got him into Ocklesford Rovers and Mr Witzel is going to help with training and act as referee. Our coach Tom does need help, but it's going to be very difficult for my trilemma if George doesn't like Stan.

While I was thinking, I kept catching up with Sibble and her friend. Sibble got cross because she thought I was spying on them. Why would I want to listen to two girls

talking about boys and nail varnish? In the end, I decided to overtake them. Sibble's even slower than usual because of her crutches By the time I got home, I was half a street ahead of Sibble and had to wait on the doorstep until she caught up and let me in because I don't have a key. (Mum says I'm not responsible enough.)

Then I discovered that I had been wasting my time on the doorstep, because Mum was already home – with a big surprise. For Sibble.

A rabbit.

My sister, who doesn't know one end of an animal from the other, has been given her own rabbit. It's from my obscure aunt in Australia, for Sibble's birthday – even though it's not Sibble's birthday for another three months. My obscure aunt told Mum to take the money

for the rabbit out of Gran's will. Mum ended up getting it from Mr Witzel, who knows all about where to get small pets from, apparently.

Then Mum told me that my obscure aunt had sent me a surprise as well. It's not my birthday either – I think my aunt just sends things at random to save her having to remember actual dates. My surprise was sent all the way from Australia and is so cool I forgot all about Sibble and her rabbit.

My present is a perspex box with an ants' nest in it. It's brilliant. You can see all the ants and what they get up to, foraging for food and building their nest. There is enough food and nest-building stuff in it to last until I'm bored and can release them into the wild. (Or into Sibble's room.)

I think Sibble was a bit upset that I wasn't jealous of her rabbit any more. She

even tried to be nice to me, by offering me some chocolate-covered raisins. Luckily I am always suspicious when Sibble gives me something, especially when she is very insistent.

Even more especially when she said she didn't want to eat them herself.

Of course she didn't. The chocolate-covered raisins were rabbit droppings.

But they have given me an idea. A cunning plan which I will carry out as soon as I can.

I went round to Stan's as soon as he was back from school football training, to show him my ants' nest. He didn't seem very interested. Besides, his mum kept interrupting our conversation.

'You sleep in the back room at home, don't you, Dougie? Have you heard any strange noises at night recently?'

I told her the noise was urban foxes and nothing to worry about.

'I didn't know foxes could climb trees,' she said. 'Our tree has got scratches all over it, like something has been trying to claw its way up. Do you know what that could be?'

'Climbing foxes?' I suggested.

Later on, Stan told me he's been picked for the school team for our next match. Billy Something-or-Other is going to be in goal instead of me. He also said that Mr Truss, who is the most boring teacher ever, is taking over the football team from Mr Goff.

But I wasn't really listening. I was wondering how I could stop the creature from climbing trees.

Then Stan said something that made me

listen. 'Why are you friends with a loser like George?'

I think I might be in my trilemma for a bit longer.

Note to my STUPID Brother: Tabitha and I thought it was VERY WEIRD, the way you kept CREEPING up behind us and muttering about Stan and George. Did you know you talk to yourself? When I told her that's nothing compared to the ODD NOISES you make when you think NO ONE is LISTENING, she thought that was EVEN weirDEr.

DEAR Dongie,

I'M GOING to LEAVE YOU my **FLUFFY CAT** AS WELL. MUM GAVE IT TO ME INSTEad of A REal ONE. I'LL Bring it round with the FLUFFY Hamster.

from Claude

FURTHER AMENDMENTS TO THE LAST WILL AND TESTAMENT OF DOUGAL TRUMP

I leave my bucket of mouldy old conkers to Claude. I'm sure he will find a good use for them.

I'm leaving these to Claude to say thank you for thinking of me in his own will, but I really don't need his fluffy toys. He doesn't seem to understand that he needs to be dead before I get them.

I, DOUGAL TRUMP, HAVE NEVER BEEN MORE WORRIED IN MY LIFE.

It's my entire family's fault.

We were sitting at the table eating Mum's brown goo when it happened. What happened was a conversation. Normally our conversations are about fascinating things like the weather, Dad's expertise in cleaning windows, Dad's desire to own a red Ferrari, Mum's interest in my homework, my interest in how she can come up with so many varieties of brown goo, all of which taste awful, Dad's disappointment in his ungrateful son, who has no idea what it is like to slave over a hot stove for your kids all day, an argument about who exactly does all the slaving over hot stoves, etc., etc.

This time the conversation went like this.

'Dougie?' said Mum. I knew at once that she was either very curious, suspicious or concerned. If she'd been nagging she'd have called me *Dougal*; if she'd been cross she'd have called me *Dougal!* with an exclamation mark.

She paused before she carried on, to make sure she had my attention. I had to cough to disguise the sound of the dog slurping the bit of brown goo I'd just given him under the table. He's recovered from his operation, and his lampshade collar is now upside down and full of fruit under my bed, along with my collection of fruit-filled arm casts.

Then Mum continued. 'Is everything all right?'

'Fine, thanks, Mum.'

'It's just that you've been behaving strangely recently,' said Mum.

'Your mother's right,' Dad mumbled through his brown goo.

'I'm not behaving strangely!' I protested, banging my fork down on the plate. Unfortunately it caught the edge and tipped the plate up, knocking Mum's brown goo all over the table. Plus some on the floor for the dog.

'Yeah, like trashing your dinner is normal,' said Sibble. 'Freak.'

I took in a big, deep breath, ready to tell Sibble what I thought of her remark. But a bit of Mum's brown goo went down the wrong way and I started choking instead. So Mum patted me on the back, a bit too hard, and her brown goo went flying out of me and straight into the dog.

'Well,' said Mum, watching me trying to shovel the brown goo back on to my plate. 'You have been acting strangely recently. Writing your will, for example. Now why would you want to do that?'

'I'm not writing my will any more,' I said. My voice was still a bit squeaky from choking. 'I've disinherited you all. For telling me I'm not normal.'

'But you have been acting strangely recently,' said Dad.

'Hello?' said Sibble. 'He's always been strange.'

'We've never known him to eat so much fruit,' said Dad. 'Even the old mouldy stuff at the bottom of the fruit bowl.'

'I haven't seen old mouldy stuff at the bottom of the fruit bowl for a long time,' said Mum.

That's because it's inside one of my arm casts, I thought.

'That's because Dougie's eaten it,' said Sibble. 'Maybe that's what's made him go weird.'

'I'm not weird!' I stood up and shouted. 'I am perfectly *normal*.' Unfortunately I still hadn't quite finished choking and the word 'normal' came out all croaky. At the same time, I coughed a bit of dribble down my chin.

'You are so not normal,' Sibble laughed up at me. 'Look at you. And I've heard you making odd noises in your room. Like this.' She started to howl and snort just like the creature in the shed does when he comes out at night. Then she started to laugh. Then Dad started to make snorting and howling noises too and then of course Mum had to join in, until they were all wiping tears of joy and laughter from their eyes.

Then the dog started running around and barking.

'Even the dog agrees!' Dad said, making them start laughing all over again.

I don't like being laughed at.

So I stood on my chair and yelled, 'STOP!'

They took no notice. So I stood on the table and yelled again.

They thought that was hysterical. So I started waving my arms about.

'It's not me making those noises,' I screamed. 'It's the creature in the shed!'

Silence. Four pairs of eyes looked up at me – Mum's, Dad's, Sibble's and the dog's.

My family think I've got an imaginary creature in the shed. My family thinks I've gone loopy.

I'm not loopy.

Am I?

Note to my STUPID brother: eventually you will go completely **MAD**. you will think you are the CREATURE in the shed and will try to eat someone. The ONLY cure will BE to shoot you and put you out of your misery (and OURS).

DEAR DOUGIE,

I'M GOING TO LEAVE YOU MY FLUFFY **DOG** AS WELL. IT'S NOT AS COOL as your dog, BUT MUM WON'T Let me have A REAL ONE. AS YOU HAVEN'T INVITED ME TO YOUR HOUSE SINCE I STARTED LEAVING you things in my will, I'LL bring it to school, along with the FLUFFY cat ~~cat~~ AND Hamster.

FROM CLAUDE

I, DOUGAL TRUMP, am in SERIOUS trouble.

I've been grounded again, until Dad says it's safe for me to come out because he's calmed down enough not to kill me. He didn't specify a method, although he did mutter something about feeding me to my imaginary creature in the shed.

It's Lysander Witzel's fault.

That's Stan's dad. Lysander. No wonder he wants everyone to call him Mr Witzel. But he's promised to make sure I'm back in goal for Ocklesford Rovers as soon as my arm is better, so I will carry on calling him Mr Witzel, even though it's his fault I'm grounded.

The only good thing about having an arm in a cast is that it makes a great clunking sound when I hit Sibble over the head with

it. But then she kicks me with her leg in its cast and that really hurts. She's stopped using crutches now and they've gone back to the hospital, which I think is really unfair – I was looking forward to having some fun with those.

Still, my cast only goes up to my elbow this time and I can use my fingers, so it wasn't too difficult to sneak into Sibble's room and collect some rabbit droppings. The rabbit, which Sibble has named Bunnykins, is

living in a cage in there until he's big enough to go outdoors. I'm very worried about this – if he goes outdoors, he'll be creature meat. Which would be a great shame as he's a nice rabbit, despite belonging to Sibble. He's little and gold and pale and fluffy with darker ears.

Anyway, I collected the droppings carefully and hid them in my room until Saturday morning, when everyone else was having a lie-in.

Before I searched Mum's might-come-in-useful drawer for what I needed next, I logged on to the computer. I put *Large hairy creature with big teeth and sharp claws* into the search engine and after a bit of whirring (our computer is very old) it came up with a yeti.

I hope it isn't a yeti. Then we're all dead.

I went to the drawer, and after a lot of rummaging I found a posh little bag with string handles, plus some pale yellow tissue paper. I carefully wrapped the droppings in the tissue and put them in the bag. The bag had a label on it which said 'Happy Birthday'. I crossed that out and, after careful thought, this is what I wrote:

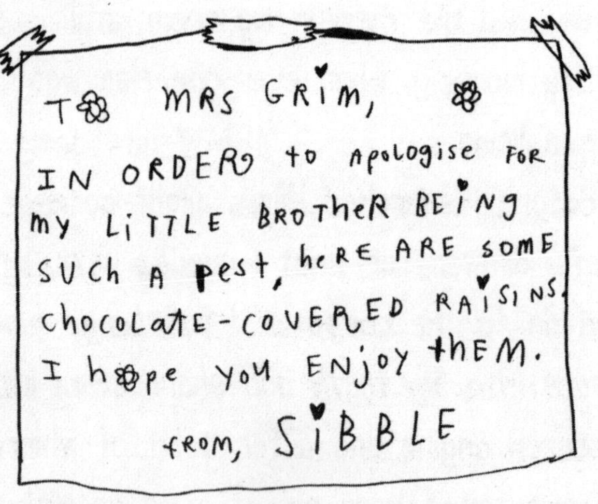

TO MRS GRIM,
IN ORDER to Apologise FOR
my LITTLE BROTheR BEING
SUCh A pest, heRE ARE SOME
chocoLate-COVERED RAISINS.
I hope you Enjoy thEM.
from, SIBBLE

I was very impressed with the note, so I read it several times. Then I took the posh bag out to the front garden. I crouched behind Mrs Grim's wall, waiting for the opportunity to deliver my gift while she wasn't looking.

Mrs Grim is always polishing her windows, or dusting the ornaments on her windowsill, or hoovering the carpet right by the window. It's virtually impossible to go past her house and not see her in the window doing something. Sometimes she just stands there, looking out. Sometimes she holds her cat by the window, so it can look out as well.

It's a big fluffy white thing that spends its days looking like a big fluffy cushion on Mrs Grim's sofa. His name is Precious.

Mrs Grim and Sibble ought to have a bad-pet-naming contest.

I was crouching by the wall when Mr Witzel came past.

'Morning, Dougie. Are you looking for something?'

'Ow!' I said, as I banged my head against the wall. 'You gave me a fright.'

'What have you got there?'

'Nothing.' I hid the bag behind my back. 'Do you know who Tom is going to play in goal instead of me while my arm is broken?'

'We're going to make a new signing,' he said. 'Someone Stan recommended. Burt Ironside.'

'Burt?' I couldn't believe it. 'Have you ever seen him play?'

'No, but I've seen him. Can't see any balls getting past him in goal, can you?'

I suppose that's true – Burt would fill the goal. But he couldn't kick a ball if it

landed on his foot. I was about to say so when Mr Witzel asked me a question that made me forget all about Burt.

'How's your shed?'

'Fine,' I said. 'Absolutely fine. Not a single yeti in it.'

At that moment Mrs Grim stuck her head out of the window and asked Mr Witzel if he'd like to have a look at her cat, as he is interested in rare breeds, apparently.

At the same time I heard a shriek from indoors that meant I was in trouble. Big trouble. I knew it was big trouble because the shriek came from Mum and contained the word '*DOUGAL!!!!!!!!*'

I never got to give the chocolate-covered raisins to Mrs Grim.

The dog had trashed the might-come-in-useful drawer. Everything was all over the

floor, the kitchen and the rest of the house – apart from what was now in the dog. Mum yelled that if the dog had to go to the vet again to have stuff removed from him, I would have to clean the car for the rest of my life to pay for it.

Then she asked what was in the little bag I was holding.

'Nothing,' I said. 'Absolutely nothing.'

That was when Sibble came in to complain about us disturbing her sleep. She snatched the bag off me, because it was her bag, in which her friend had given her a present two years ago for her birthday.

Then she saw what was in the bag and showed Mum. Who showed Dad.

'It's obvious you wrote the note,' said Sibble. 'I know how to spell my own name.'

'It wasn't my idea!' I said, which was

true, as Sibble had originally put the idea in my head.

'Don't tell me,' said Dad. 'It was the mystery creature, giving you strange ideas.'

'Yeah,' giggled Sibble. 'It probably crept out of the shed last night, climbed through Dougie's window and whispered in his ear while he was sleeping.'

'Or maybe Dougie just went to the shed to ask the creature advice about how to drive his mother mad,' said Mum.

'Maybe we should go and have a word with this creature,' said Dad.

I tried not to imagine that conversation:

HAVE YOU BEEN GIVING MY SON STRANGE IDEAS?
YOU LOOK GOOD ENOUGH TO EAT.

'OK,' I said. 'It was me. It was my idea. But Sibble started it, when she tried to give me chocolate-covered raisins.'

'That was very nice of Sibble,' said Mum.

Before I could correct myself and explain that Sibble had tried to give me rabbit droppings, Dad ordered me to clean the car – inside and out. And before I could object, Mum produced the waterproof protector for my arm cast and started forcing it on.

'But I haven't had breakfast yet!' I protested.

'You can have breakfast when you've washed the car,' said Dad.

So I went out to wash the car.

And that's when the trouble really started.

It's the dog's fault, really.

I had to leave the front door open so

I could plug the Hoover in. Immediately, the stupid cat ran out of the house, chased by the dog. It's not my fault the stupid cat jumped over Mrs Grim's wall, followed by the dog, who started running round and round her front garden, looking for the cat, who was hiding in a bush.

I had to go after the dog. I chased him round and round and he sprayed gravel everywhere. He thought it was great fun and began to bark. Mrs Grim came out.

That's when the cat sneaked out from under the bush and dashed into Mrs Grim's house. The dog then followed the cat into her house, bringing his muddy paws with him, and a heap of wet gravel. He banged into the telephone table and knocked a vase of flowers off it, which smashed and spilt water everywhere.

Mrs Grim was still screaming at me when I got the dog by the collar and dragged him out. I don't know why she was so angry at me, when in actual fact I'd just saved her from a highly crazed dog. She should be grateful that the dog hadn't gone near her precious Precious.

Also, Mrs Grim shouldn't be so afraid of mice. She should have a proper cat to deal with them. Then she wouldn't have been so frightened by the one she found when she was clearing up the mess. Her shriek was loud enough for the whole street to hear. She came running round to our house in a fury, accusing me of leaving the mouse under the telephone table.

I don't know how she knew it was me. It's not my fault I accidentally left it there last time I went round to get my football,

as she distracted me by saying that was the last time she would ever let me collect my ball – ever. She says that every time.

It's not my fault Mrs Grim didn't look where she was going when she came stomping up our drive to tell on me. It's not my fault she fell over the Hoover which I had been using to helpfully clean the car.

Uncle William came straight round and, after examining her, told Mrs Grim that she had broken her leg. At this point I decided to give them all some space.

Then Dad came upstairs and told me what he was going to do instead of killing me.

NOTE TO THE POLICE:

if I have died of BOREDOM, It will be because Dad grounded me for THREE WEEKS!

If I have died because of ~~embarrassment~~ EMBARRASSMENT that will be because Claude brought a small collection of FLUFFY toys to school for me.

Leabharlanna Poibli Chathair Baile Átha Cliath
Dublin City Public Libraries

I, DOUGAL TRUMP, AM ALIVE, BUT GROUNDED.

No football, no PlayStation, no TV, no nothing. All I'm allowed to do is my homework and tidy my room – the two most boring things in the world, apart from washing the car, which I'm still forced to do for free. For some reason I don't have to hoover it any more though.

I'm only allowed out of my room to go to school. I have to walk straight to school with Stan, or get a lift in his mum's new car, and I have to come straight back with Stan or Sibble without going round to Claude's or George's first. Claude and George go round to Billy Something-or-Other's house anyway – they seem to have

got very friendly with him very quickly.

Stan is now friends with Burt Ironside, of all people. He comes home with Stan sometimes and I have to be careful he doesn't tread on me while I'm walking with them.

At school I thought that I might get a break from people feeling disappointed in me. But no. Mr Truss, the most boring teacher in the world, made me stay in at break so he could give me a long talk, telling me that I should think about the consequences of my actions.

I didn't think there was much point in telling him it wasn't my fault.

When he'd finished, he asked me if there was anything I'd like to say to him.

'Yes, there is something, Mr Truss,' I said. 'Do you know what sort of creature is

big, hairy, has large claws, sharp teeth, eats compost heaps, bucketloads of fruit (skins and all), climbs trees, goes down bins and makes funny noises at night?'

'DOUGAL TRUMP!!!!

!!!!!!!!!!!!!!!!!!

!!!!!!!!!!!!!!!!!!

!!!!!!!!!!!!!!!!!

!!!!!!!!!!!!!!!!!

!!!!!!!!!!!!!!!!'

he replied, with a whole page full of exclamation marks. 'This is no time for a joke! You can stay in at break for the rest of the week!'

I am grounded at school as well.

DOUGIE,

OF COURSE CLAUDE AND ME WILL KEEP GETTING FRUIT TO THE CREATURE WHILE YOU ARE GROUNDED AGAIN.

AND BILLY AS WELL. I THINK STAN TOLD BURT ABOUT IT. I TOLD YOU NOT TO TRUST HIM.

- GEORGE

PS. EAT THIS NOTE.

Dougie,

I'll keep quiet about the creature in the shed if you do my English homework for me.

- STAN

Dougie,

Well done for getting
a merit for your history
project about the origins
of football.
I liked the bit about
kicking your enemies' heads
around. I hope you don't
have to be grounded at home
and kept in at school break
before you do the next piece
of good work.

LOVE, MUM

DOUGIE,

Burt will KEEP quiet ABOUT
the creature in the shed
if you do **ALL** his
homework For him.

-STAN

Dear Dougie,

i will try and do all of your homework for you, BUT i CAN'T Do Stan and Burt's as well, Because i Need time to find fruit for the creature in the shed. i will ASK Billy, He's MUCH CLEVERER than me.

from CLAUDE.

DEAR DOUGIe,

Thanks for letting me see your creature. It is very interesting. DO you know what it is? I COULD find out FOR YOU if YOU'D Like. SORRY, I am unable to DO any homeWORK FOR YOU, My DAD will go mental.

-BiLLY T.

Note to my Disgusting BROTHER: Angela Sweeter's brother Eric is in my class and he says your friends keep going on about the creature in our shed. PLEASE STOP - it's getting EMBARRASSING NOW.

Thanks for getting a merit for my story about a football team with a boy whose dad is a dodgy referee, which i had to read out loud in class. But make sure you don't write such good stories for Burt - he needs to understand all the words you use.

Regards, Stan

DEAR DOUGIE,

I Don't think the creature is a YETI. Yetis eat Rhododendrons and, as you said, it hasn't eaten Mrs GRIM's Rhododendrons yet.

- BILLY T

DOUGAL,

This STORY ABOUT A CREATURE IN THE SHED WOULD HAVE BEEN BETTER IF IT HAD BEEN MORE BELIEVABLE.

I KNOW YOU CAN DO BETTER. HAVE A LOOK AT STAN WITZEL'S STORY - THAT IS WHAT YOU SHOULD BE AIMING FOR.

MR TRUSS

PS - I COULDN'T HELP NOTICING THAT BURT'S HANDWRITING WAS JUST LIKE YOURS IN THE STORY HE HANDED IN, ABOUT A LARGE BOY WHO COULDN'T KICK A FOOTBALL IF IT LANDED ON HIS FOOT.

Burt is cross because he got into trouble. It's your fault because you forgot to write like him. But don't worry, I stopped him from being angry with you by telling him he CAN stay in goal for Ocklesford Rovers even when your arm is out of its cast.

– Stan

NotE to my STUPID BROthER: I am **NOT** ugly, my legs arE **NOT** hairy and i DO **NOT** have a boyfriend !!!!

I'M CUTTING SOME fruit up so the CREature can put it ON his claws like BALOO the Bear Does in Jungle Book. -CLAUDE

mum said she keeps hearing scratching and grunting noises outside at night. she said she saw something in our garden last night. Dad said she dreamt the whole thing. You owe me another story for keeping Quiet about what's REALLY out there. DON'T worry, I will copy out your story in my OWN HANDwriting.

AND i will tell mrs GRim that the disappearance of Her cat had Nothing to Do with you. You OWE me, BIG TiME.

- STAN

DOUGIE,

I HAVE DECIDED TO LEAVE OCKLESFORD ROVERS AND GO AND PLAY FOR FAIRFORD UNITED.

- GEORGE

NOTE TO WHOEVER LEFT THE CREATURE IN THE SHED.

I am very WORRIED BECAUSE it has BEEN IN there FOR A FEW WEEKS NOW. YOU WERE Supposed TO COLLECT it BEFORE IT WOKE UP AND it has BEEN **VERY MUCH** AWAKE and PEOPLE ARE getting SUSPICIOUS.

I CAN'T KEEP PRETENDING it's ME making ~~[illegible]~~ FUNNY NOISES, BECAUSE EVERYONE thinks I'VE gone **LOOPY.**

MRS GRIM'S cat has DISAPPEARED. YOU SAID the CREATURE ATE FRUIT BUT DOES it EAT CATS TOO?

HAS the CREATURE EATEN **YOU**?

YOURS ANXIOUSLY,

DOUGAL TRUMP

I, DOUGAL TRUMP, HAVE BEEN BETRAYED BY MY BEST FRIEND.

George has gone to play for Fairford United! Even worse, Tom the coach has gone with him. How could they? It's the worst team ever. It's got Claude in it. And Billy Something-or-Other is their goalie.

Luckily I have also had some good news. I AM GETTING A ROOM IN THE LOFT!

Some of the money from Gran's will is going to pay for a room in our loft and Mum and Dad have decided that I can have it as my bedroom. I can't wait. But that meant the loft needed clearing out. And guess where Dad wanted to put all the stuff?

'You can't put it in the shed!' I said.

'Why not?' said Dad. 'Worried your creature might object?'

'It leaks,' I said. 'And it might fall down on you and ruin all the stuff.'

'I don't think that would matter,' said Mum. 'It's mostly junk anyway.'

'It's not junk!' protested Dad. 'There's some good stuff up there.'

'You could just throw it all in the skip,' said Mum.

'Great idea,' I said.

'I am not throwing good stuff away in the skip!' said Dad.

'I know!' I said, thinking quickly. 'You can put all the stuff in my room.' They both looked doubtfully at me. 'That'll save you from the effort of taking it all the way to the shed, won't it, Dad?'

'And it means he still won't fix the leaky roof,' said Mum.

Luckily Dad won that argument and the

creature is still safe. And I'm still alive.

My room is now so full of stuff that I can hardly move. This includes fifteen bin-liners of Gran's stuff, plus six suitcases, two trunks, eight cardboard boxes and several other pieces of dusty, cobweb-covered junk from the loft.

I've had some fun rummaging around in the stuff from the loft and found all sorts of interesting items, including:

* A box full of old vinyl records, which are black, round, plastic things that can apparently play music and were what people used before CDs, iPods and downloads were invented.

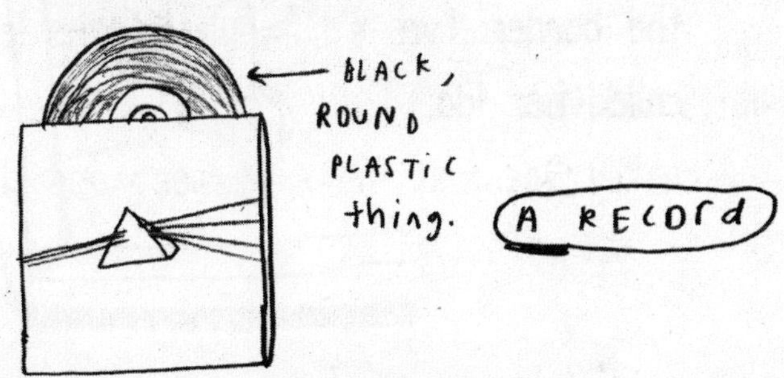

* Several tins of paint, with lids stuck on, so that I can't remove them even when I bang them with a hammer. A box of tools, including the hammer and several unidentifiable metal objects, sections of plastic pipes, tins of goo, bits of wire, rusty screwdrivers, old plugs, a thousand screws of assorted sizes and several bits of wood, all left over from Dad's failed DIY projects.

* Thirteen revolting paintings, very dusty and old-looking. One of them has an enormous spider living in the corner. I've called her Ida.

* The Stamford United programme from when Dad took me to a match. It's in a terrible mess, after Dad kept rolling it up and unrolling it, chewed the end off, threw it up in the air when Stamford United scored and then jumped on it when Arsenal equalized. Luckily the score was 1-1, or the programme wouldn't have survived at all.

* Some old toys that I used to play with (apparently), including a Thomas the Tank Engine train set, complete with fourteen trains, two miles of track, three stations and one Fat Controller; a ton of Duplo bricks; four Action Man dolls (I don't think they were mine); several broken remote-control cars and a big pile of dusty books.

Most of the books are about football and very old. Inside each one, Dad has written:

THIS BOOK BELONGS TO RAYMOND TRUMP, SOON TO BE THE NEW STAR OF STAMFORD UNITED.

He used to have big dreams in his younger years.

One of the books is called *How to Be a Good Referee.* I think I should give it to Lysander Witzel, because he's not as good a referee as he thinks he is. He blows his whistle every time his son Stan wants the ball and either gives him a free kick or a penalty. Stan only has to go down clutching his ankle and he gets a free kick. One time, he even clutched the wrong ankle.

I'm beginning to wonder whether George

was right when he told me not to trust Stan. I've found out that he doesn't even support Stamford United.

The last dusty old box I looked in had a sewing machine in it. It also had some scraps of material, so I thought I'd see if I could get the sewing machine to work. It was a bit tricky with one arm in a cast, but I managed it.

Then I did a very good job of sewing my finger up.

Mum heard me yelling and came rushing in to find me wrestling with her old sewing machine, trying to get my finger out.

'Raymond!' she shouted for Dad. 'Come and see what your son has done now!'

I heard Dad muttering all the way up the stairs. 'This had better be good. The match is about to start.'

'Never mind the match,' said Mum. 'Apart from making a terrible mess with all your stuff from the loft, which you wouldn't put in the shed because you couldn't be bothered to fix it, your son has ruined my sewing machine.'

'How come he's always *my* son when he's done something stupid?' said Dad. 'Perhaps you should have thrown your sewing machine out.'

'I'm not throwing my sewing machine out,' she said. 'You should throw all this junk out.'

While they were arguing, I managed to get my finger out of the sewing machine, by

turning the handle up so the needle came out. Along with a lot of blood. Which went everywhere.

'Now look what he's done!' said Mum.

That's when the dog came bounding into my bedroom. Unfortunately, he found my collection of fruit-filled casts under my bed. I tried to grab him at the same time Dad did.

'You've got blood on my T-shirt now!' said Dad. Luckily he didn't notice that he'd just trodden on an old banana.

I was now playing tug-of-war with the dog and getting blood all over the cast as well. But I was more worried about more fruit falling out of it. Then Mum took the dog by the collar and shut him out of the room.

'Raymond,' said Mum, ignoring the scratching and whining from the other side of my door, 'I think we'd better take Dougie

to hospital to have his finger looked at.'

They both looked at my finger, which was still dripping. They didn't notice me shove the cast back under my bed with my foot.

'Do we have to?' said Dad. 'It's only a scratch. And the match is about to start.'

Mum gave him one of her looks.

'OK, tell you what,' said Dad. 'If it hasn't stopped bleeding by the time the match has finished, I'll take him.'

I looked at my finger. 'I might not have any blood left by then.'

'Take him now,' said Mum.

'You take him,' said Dad.

After a bit of arguing, during which I wrapped some of the cloth that came with the sewing machine round my finger, they both took me to A & E. Dad managed to lose the banana off his foot as he went downstairs. He didn't notice, but he did wonder why the dog was licking the stairs as we left.

'Hello, again,' said the nurse in A & E. 'What have you done this time?'

I now have a cast on one arm and a big bandage round my finger on the other hand. It's great. It means I don't have to do any writing at school.

Note to my stupid Brother: please, please could you give us all a break and feed yourself to the creature in the shed?

I, Dougal TRUMP, am very WORRiED. VERY WORRiED iNDEED.

It's the creature's fault. And Mum and Dad's. And I'm pretty sure it's Sibble's fault as well.

A while ago, Mum and Dad agreed (they do agree sometimes) that it's safe for me to walk home from school over the Ockle Fields. That's as long as I walk with George and Claude and don't leave them until we get to my street. My street is not dangerous – apart from the odd creature who might come out of a shed and eat you.

And that is what's really worrying me.

I was walking across the fields with George and Claude, trying to persuade George to come back to Ocklesford Rovers, when we

passed the hollow tree near the river. It's got a big hole in it, where we used to hide when we were children.

As we walked past the hollow tree George and I stopped, because we'd noticed something. (Claude carried on, because he never notices anything.) What we noticed was a series of scratches all around the hollow bit of the tree. We looked at each other without saying anything. Then we grinned because, despite being in opposing football teams, we both had the same idea at the same time.

Something with big claws had been scratching the hollow tree.

Something with big claws hoping to find some fruit?

Claude realized we'd stopped and came back. Then he pointed out the poster on the hollow tree:

There was a photo of a small dog with no hair, apart from an orange tuft between its sticky-up ears. I've never seen such an ugly dog. No wonder it's rare.

It's not the only notice I've seen. There's one in our road for a rare fluffy rabbit that has gone missing from someone's garden.

And another one about a large, fluffy, white rare-breed cat called Precious.

I think I know why these animals keep vanishing.

Maybe if we leave extra fruit in the hollow tree, the creature will stop eating pets.

But I'm still worried. I don't want the creature to eat my hamster. Or the cat. Even the dog. And I definitely don't want it eating me.

I don't mind if it eats Sibble.

Note to my STUPID BROTHER: STOP going ON about the CREATURE in the shed, it's getting boring. AS soon as Dad finds the key, he's going in there to PROVE that you ARE

MAD.

FURTHER AMENDMENTS TO THE LAST WILL AND TESTAMENT OF DOUGAL TRUMP

The bag of sand and seashells which I brought back from holiday last year I leave to Mum. She is always saying she wishes she was lying on a beach somewhere instead of in this madhouse. I thought she could lie down on her bed with the bag open, with the smell of the sea wafting over her.

I leave this to her for telling Sibble to stop going on about me going on about the creature in the shed. She says the joke is wearing a bit thin.

To Claude I leave the dog. That is the closest I can get to giving him back the fluffy animals, which are now inside the dog.

I, Dougal TRUMP, REALLY AM DEAD This TIME. VERY, VERY DEAD. VERY DEAD INDEED. This is my FINAL FAREWELL.

Something terrible has happened. Something very terrible indeed. I am in the biggest, hugest, freakiest trouble ever.

This time it really isn't my fault – but I know I'll never be able to prove it.

And to make things worse, Dad has found the key to the shed.

He is going to go down to the even wilder end of the garden, where he hasn't been in years, open up the shed and prove to everyone that I am loopy. He's going to rush in there and say something like –

HELLO, CREATURE!
HERE COMES DOUGIE'S DADDY!

with a big grin on his face. Thinking he's funny. Thinking he won't find a creature in the shed. Oh dear.

Perhaps it's just as well. After what has happened, no way do George, Claude and Billy want to be my friends any more. No way will they feed the creature for me now.

I am friendless. I am creatureless.

I'm going to miss the creature. Even if it does eat my dad.

It all began just after I went to hospital to have my cast off. At the same time I had the big bandage on my finger

changed for a smaller one. Dad took Mrs Grim as well, to have her leg looked at.

Mrs Grim had her leg cast sawn off, only to have another one put on. She had to have her cast redone because they changed their minds.

Then the same thing happened to Sibble!

Sibble's new cast is like a big boot. I have to keep clear of her, as it can deliver an almighty kick.

Then her rabbit disappeared and everyone thinks it was me.

It is true that I thought her rabbit would like running along Mrs Grim's old plaster cast for a bit of fun, before I filled it up with fruit. But no way did I take Bunnykins out of his hutch and forget to put him back again.

I can't tell them that the creature must

have eaten Sibble's rabbit. They'd think I'd gone loopy.

I don't think I've got time to make another will, so the last one will stand. That means everyone is disinherited apart from Claude and George. But, after what happened, I don't think they will want anything from me.

I think I had better plan my funeral instead.

INSTRUCTIONS REGARDING THE FUNERAL OF

Dougal TRUMP

I have decided that, as well as the usual funeral, I should have a memorial service, at King's Road football ground, home of Stamford United, the best team in the world. My coffin must be placed in the centre of the pitch, covered in my Stamford United duvet cover.

I know a lot of people will wish to stand up and say what a marvellous person I was. Here are some guidelines about what they might like to say:

MUM:

I can't possibly make a speech – I'm crying too much! I wish I hadn't made him tidy up his

room – I'd give anything to be able knee high in all that lovely mess!

MUM'S TEARDROPS

Could someone pass me a tissue, please?

DAD:

Dougie was the best son ever. He was very brave when I kicked a penalty so hard that it broke his arm for the first time (or was it the second?). He was brilliant at football and I'll miss our kick-arounds, although he was getting far too good for me.

The PlayStation isn't the same without Dougie to beat me at every game we play. He was the best car washer who ever lived. I should have paid him double. I should never have given him all those unfair groundings.

SIBBLE:

I wish I hadn't made such a fuss. It's only a broken leg and I've got a perfectly good other one.

UNCLE WILLIAM:

I wish I had shown more interest in Dougie's broken arms. I'm now convinced (too late) that he had a remarkable bone structure.

MR TRUSS:

Dougie was our star pupil. He was so bright that we should never have made him do any work. I should never have kept him in at break-times.

LYSANDER WITZEL:

Dougie was the best goalie I've ever seen. He was far too good for my team, Ocklesford Rovers, and I should have played him as soon as his arm was better, instead of keeping Burt Ironside, who fills the goal but is hopeless.

I admit to being a cheat and a useless coach. I hereby resign as manager of Ocklesford Rovers.

MRS GRIM:

I couldn't have hoped for a better neighbour than Dougal Trump. He brightened up my life and living next to him brought something new every day.

Dougal filled my life with wonder; he filled my garden with footballs; he filled my greenhouse with holes; he filled in the mystery holes in my lawn. I know he had nothing to do with the disappearance of my precious cat – who is called Precious.

GEORGE QUICKLY:

Dougie was my best mate and like another brother to me. He would have been my sixth or seventh brother, I think. I can't remember how many brothers I have.

I'm sorry I left Ocklesford Rovers, but I couldn't stand Stan Witzel and that smarmy father of his. They are such cheats.

CLAUDE BARLEYCORN:

Has the creature gone now? I've got a banana for it.

BILLY SOMETHING-OR-OTHER:

Oh dear.

STAN WITZEL:

I request to be put in the coffin and cremated with Dougie. Alive.

THE CAT:

Miaow!

THE HAMSTER:

Nibble, nibble.

THE DOG:

Yum, this coffin tastes good. The corners are particularly good for gnawing on.

THE CREATURE in the SHED:

Sorry for keeping you awake at night with my funny noises. Sorry for eating Mrs Grim's cat. And Sibble's rabbit. And the other small animals that have gone missing.

Why are you all screaming and running away?

YIPPEE – he's DEAD!!! PEACE at LAST – hooray!!

P.S. – HE WON'T have MOURNERS – he'll have CHEERLEADERS.

P.P.S. – I wish he wouldn't KEEP going on about his imaginary creature in the shed. And Blaming it for eating my Rabbit is horrible.

FOR what it's WORTH I, DOUGAL TRUMP, HEREBY EXPLAIN what HAPPENED TO MAKE **ME** GROUNDED FOREVER.

I hope that someone, someday, will believe me.

The hamster started it.

If he hadn't escaped from his cage and run along my windowsill at completely the wrong moment, none of this would have happened. Then the cat wouldn't have jumped on to my windowsill, thinking he might have a hamster-burger for his tea. But the hamster ran for his life and hid behind the first thing he found – the ants' nest from my obscure aunt in Australia.

I'd given the ants names – Ant 1, Ant 2, Ant 3, Ant 4, Ant 5, Ant 6, Ant 7, Ant 8,

Ant 9 and all the way to Ant 196, when I had to stop counting because they were moving around and I thought I'd counted some of them twice. Their nest was coming along nicely.

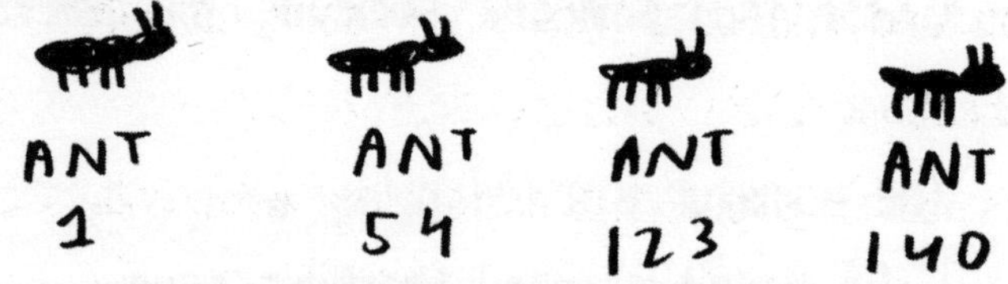

The cat followed the hamster and knocked the ants' nest on to the floor. It didn't burst open, but the ants got very antsy.

Then the stupid dog bounded into my bedroom to see what was going on. As soon as he saw me rushing to pick up the ants' nest, he decided that the ants' nest was the only thing in the world he wanted. He beat me to it and ran off with it clamped between his jaws. I chased him along the landing and cornered him outside Sibble's closed door. It has a notice on it which says *Dougie, if you open this door, you will die.*

As I was playing tug-of-war with the dog and the ants' nest, the door opened behind me.

Sibble stood there gawping, with only a towel wrapped around her. The dog ran straight through her legs and she dropped the towel. I shielded my face and closed my eyes – very tightly.

It was a few seconds before the shrieking Sibble wriggled back into her towel and I could open my eyes again. That is when the unbreakable perspex cracked open in the dog's jaws. He dropped half of the nest and ran round Sibble's room with the other half. There isn't much space in Sibble's room, so

he went in crazy small circles, which made it impossible to chase him.

Then Sibble felt an ant on her bare foot.

Then she felt it on her calf.

Then she felt it behind her knee.

Then she felt it on her thigh.

Then she realized that they were all different ants.

Then Mum was upstairs screaming even louder than Sibble. She blamed me for the fact that Sibble's room was now crawling with ants. Then she put me in their bedroom because it has a lock. And locked me in.

She said I was in even bigger trouble than I was already in. I hadn't realized I was already in trouble, but didn't have the heart ask her what that trouble was.

The builders have put a skip under my parents' bedroom window. This is about the

only thing they have done so far. They've already filled it up – with stuff that looked like it would make a reasonable landing if someone jumped on to it from a bedroom window. They've managed to do this without the aid of their plank, which they accused me of stealing – several times.

Why would I want to steal their plank?

My landing wasn't as soft as I hoped. But Mum and Sibble were still hopping around upstairs, so they didn't hear me crash.

Luckily I didn't break anything. My bones, I mean; I'm sure I broke lots of stuff in the skip.

I, DOUGAL TRUMP, **CURSE** the DAY STAN WITZEL MOVED IN NEXT DOOR.

I thought we were friends.

'What are you doing in the skip?' he asked, when he found me in the skip.

'Escaping.'

'But you're not grounded any more.'

'I know, but I still had to escape,' I said. 'Can't you hear all that screaming upstairs?'

'Oh. What have you done this time?'

'Nothing!' And I told him about Sibble's legs and the ants' nest.

When he'd finished laughing, he asked me if I wanted to go to the river with him.

'I can't,' I said. 'I'm not allowed to go there on my own.'

'You won't be on your own, you'll be with me.'

On the way there, I got him to promise that he'd have a word with his dad about making sure I was back as Ocklesford Rovers' goalie as soon as possible. By the time we arrived, I was feeling very happy.

Then I saw who was waiting for us next to the hollow tree by the river: Burt Ironside. I hoped Stan wasn't going to tell him that I was replacing him as Ocklesford Rovers' goalie. Not while I was there.

'I've got Dougie,' announced Stan. 'I said I'd bring him, didn't I?'

'Thank you, Stan,' said Burt. 'Hello, Dougie.'

'Hello, Burt,' I said.

'All we need now is George,' said Stan.

'Oh yes,' said Burt, looking at the ground – which is quite a long way down for him.

'Dougie, you know where George lives, don't you?' said Stan. I nodded. 'Go and get him.'

'Why?' I asked. 'What's going on here anyway?'

'You want him back in Ocklesford Rovers, don't you? Tell him you've got a big surprise for him, and when he gets here we'll persuade him to come back. Then we can all be friends playing for the same team. What do you think?'

'OK. What's the big surprise I'm supposed to have for him?'

'If I tell you, it won't be a surprise.'

So off I went to George's house. I was already there when I realized I shouldn't have gone on my own. But I survived.

I banged on George's door and one of his many brothers opened it. I went straight

in and there, sitting around the television and eating crisps, were George, Claude and Billy Something-or-Other. They looked at me guiltily.

'Sorry we didn't invite you,' said George. 'We thought you were still grounded.'

'Never mind,' I said. 'I've got a surprise for you, George. On the meadow. By the hollow tree.'

'What's the surprise?'

'If I tell you, it won't be a surprise. I'll race you!'

George can't resist a race. He ran straight out of his house, with me running after him. Billy and Claude stopped to put their trainers back on first. George can run surprisingly fast for a skinny boy in bare feet and, because I was already tired from running to his house, he got to the river before I did.

That's when Stan and Burt leaped out from behind the hollow tree. Burt grabbed hold of George, in a bear hug.

'Surprise!' yelled Stan.

I sprinted up to them. 'Why are you holding George like that?' I panted.

'Stan told me to,' said Burt.

George was struggling so much I don't think he heard. 'Is this supposed to be your surprise?' he shouted, looking straight at me.

I looked at Stan in confusion. Stan

grinned at me. 'Nice one, Dougie. OK, Burt?'

I absolutely can't believe what happened next. Stan dragged something up from the top of the bank. A plank. And not just any plank.

'Hey!' I recognized it. 'That's our builders' plank! They think I stole it!'

'Keep your hair on, Dougie, they can have it back. Just as soon as George has walked it. Isn't that right, Burt?' Stan grinned at Burt. Then he pushed the plank out, so the end of it hovered over the bank. Burt pushed George on to the other end and held him there.

'Now,' said Stan, 'Burt will stand here to hold down the plank. George will walk to the end of it and then jump into the river.'

'Why?' I asked. But no one heard me because George was shouting at me.

Something about being the worst friend in the world.

'This is to teach George a lesson for telling Mr Truss that Billy should always have first place as goalie in the school football team,' continued Stan. 'And for saying that Burt shouldn't even be considered.'

'It's not up to me!' George screamed. 'Billy is a better goalie than Burt. Even Dougie is better than Burt – everyone knows that.'

I didn't think that was a very sensible thing to say, seeing as Burt was right behind him. And holding him on the plank.

'Let go of me!' George struggled.

Burt let go of George and stepped off the plank. George and the plank tipped forward and fell into the river.

I, DOUGAL TRUMP, REALLY DON'T WANT TO REMEMBER WHAT HAPPENED NEXT.

Billy Something-or-Other arrived and waded straight into the river to help George. He tripped and ended up sitting in the water next to George, who was looking very cross. I thought I'd better go down there and explain.

But my dad got there first.

I hadn't noticed that Lysander Witzel and my dad were charging over until it was too late.

When our dads asked what was going on, Stan blamed me.

'Dougie said he wanted to give George a surprise,' he said, wide-eyed and looking as horrified as our dads. 'I didn't know what he was planning.'

Mrs Minns should give him the main part in the next school play.

'But–' was all I managed to say before Billy Something-or-Other came out of the river, holding his arm and moaning in pain.

That was when Claude arrived. (He doesn't run as fast as the rest of us.)

Claude told Dad and Lysander that I'd gone to George's house when they were in the middle of watching some cool DVD. He said I made George run out without any trainers because I had a surprise for him at the hollow tree by the river. He then asked me whether the surprise was a load of creature babies in the hollow tree.

Dad stopped me from throwing Claude in the river. I don't think he heard what Claude said, but he did give the tree a long look. He even went up to it and had a closer look at the scratches on it. Luckily he was then distracted by George. Unluckily George was

scrambling up the bank, holding the builders' plank, which Dad recognized immediately. George flung the plank down and stood there covered in mud to thank me in a very cross voice for his so-called surprise. Dad and I were still staring speechlessly at the plank (me because my mouth wouldn't work properly and only a funny little squeak came out, and Dad because he was actually speechless) when Lysander Witzel spoke.

'Why don't you come home with me now, Stan?' He put his arm around Stan, as if to protect him from me. 'I don't think you want to have any more to do with Dougal Trump from now on.' He gave me a filthy look. Then he gave Dad a filthy look. 'You should learn to control your son,' he said. As he led Stan away, we heard him say, 'Remind me to tell your mum to get another window cleaner.' And

then, more softly as they got further away: 'And Dougie won't be playing for Ocklesford Rovers any more either.'

'Wait!' I yelled. I tried to run after them, but Dad held me back. 'Don't you want to know the real story?'

Lysander Witzel stopped. He turned round. 'Go on then, if you must.'

Dad folded his arms. He does that when he's really fed up.

I started to blurt out the truth, but it didn't come out very well. It sort of sounded like this:

WELL IT WAS THE DOG AND THE CAT AND THEN THE ANTS AND SIBBLE'S LEG AND THEN IT WAS THE HAMSTER, NO IT WAS THE HAMSTER FIRST AND THEN I HAD TO JUMP IN THE SKIP AND STAN...

That was as far as I got. Stan was standing behind his dad making clawing gestures with his hands and gnashing movements with his mouth, licking his lips and miming a belch followed by a vomit. I think he was trying to tell me something – either that he'd tell his dad about the creature in the shed, or he was threatening to feed me to it. Either way, I became so confused I stopped talking.

Besides, Dad interrupted me. 'Come on, Dougie, we all know what happened and even you couldn't find an excuse for this one.'

Then Mr Truss turned up.

My teacher. Turning up to see me in the biggest trouble ever. What on earth was he doing there?

That was when I learned what Billy's

surname is. It's not Something-or-Other. It's Truss.

Billy Truss.

Mr Truss is Billy's dad!!

And Billy was standing there, wet, muddy and clutching his arm like he'd broken it and telling Mr Truss that I had tricked George into coming to the river and getting Burt Ironside to make him walk the plank.

That was when I noticed Burt wasn't there. I have no idea how he sneaked off, being so big, but he'd vanished without a trace.

So there was only me left to take the blame.

I think I'm going to have to stay in at break until I'm ninety.

DEAR HAMSTER,
IF YOU EVER ESCAPE FROM YOUR CAGE AGAIN, I WILL FEED YOU TO THE CAT.

DEAR CAT,
IF YOU EVER COME INTO MY ROOM AGAIN I'LL FEED YOU TO THE DOG.

DEAR DOG,
IF YOU EVER COME INTO MY ROOM AGAIN, I WILL FEED YOU TO THE CREATURE IN THE SHED.

DEAR DAD,
WHY DON'T YOU EVER LISTEN TO ME? IT WASN'T MY FAULT! WHY DID YOU LISTEN TO LYSANDER AND STAN, WHEN THEY ARE BOTH BIG LIARS?

~~DID YOU KNOW YOUR EYEBROWS~~

DID YOU KNOW THAT YOUR EYEBROWS WAGGLE WHEN YOU'RE ANGRY?

DEAR BUILDERS,
I DIDN'T STEAL THE PLANK!

DEAR MR TRUSS,

IF I HAVE to stay in at BREAK FOR THE REST OF MY LIFE, COULD YOU GIVE ME SOMEthing INTERESTING to DO FOR A CHANGE?

DEAR STAN,

I NEVER WANT TO TALK TO You AGAIN. I DIDN'T take ANY NOTICE OF You WHEN I SAW YOU IN YOUR GARDEN just NOW, LOOKING UP at MY WINDOW Making FLUTTERING MOVEMENTS with your FINGERS. I have NO iDEA what you MEAN AND You Look LIKE A GIRL.

DEAR BILLY,

I DIDN'T KNOW MR TRUSS WAS YOUR DAD. I CAN SEE WHY YOU DIDN'T MENTION it - he's A BIT DULL, ISN'T HE? I'M SORRY YOU BROKE YOUR ARM.

DEAR GEORGE,

YOU WErE right ABOUT STAN.
HE'S A Big LiAR AND NOT TO
BE TRUSTED. YOU PROBABLY DON'T
WANT to talk to ME EVEr Again,
BUT iF I GiVE YOU Mrs GRiM'S LEG
CAST, COULD YOU GiVE thE CREATURE
ONE LAST MEAL FROM thE FRUit
iN it, then put it ON and
GiVE STAN and BURT A [kick]
FROM ME?

NOW THAT TOM is COACH AT
FAiRFORD UNiTED, COULD YOU
ASK HiM iF HE NEEDS A
NEW GOALiE, SINCE BiLLY HAS
BROKEN His ARM AFTER FALLiNg
IN tHE RiVER?

AND PLEASE, PLEASE CARRY ON
PUTTiNg FRUiT iN thE HOLLOW
TREE FOR ThE CREatURE.

FAREWELL my FRiEND.

DEAR BURT,

STOP HANGING AROUND OUR HOUSE AND TRYING TO CALL ON ME WHEN YOU KNOW I'M GROUNDED AND it's YOUR FAULT. AND STOP TAPPING ON THE LIVING-ROOM WINDOW WHEN I'VE SNEAKED DOWNSTAIRS. YOU LOOK VERY SILLY STANDING OUTSIDE FLUTTERING YOUR HANDS IN THE AIR LIKE A GREAT BIG GIRL. YOU AND STAN HAVE OBVIOUSLY CAUGHT SOME STRANGE HAND-FLUTTERING DISEASE AND I SUGGEST YOU BOTH SEEK TREATMENT IMMEDIATELY.

DEAR CLAUDE,

SORRY ABOUT THE FRUIT FROM MY CASTS LANDING ON YOUR HEAD WHEN I TIPPED IT OUT OF MY WINDOW FOR YOU TO FEED THE CREATURE.

DEAR MRS GRIM,
I SAW YOU IN THE BACK
GARDEN WITH THE MAN FROM
THE COUNCIL, COMPLAINING
ABOUT THE DAMAGE THE
FOXES WERE DOING TO YOUR
GARDEN. IT'S NOT THE
FOXES.

DEAR BUILDERS,
I'VE just kicked my FOOTBALL
through MY BEDROOM WINDOW. DO
YOU THINK YOU COULD STOP
DRINKING TEA AND FIX IT
BEFORE MY DAD NOTICES? YOU
DON'T SEEM TO BE DOING ANY
other WORK SO I'M SURE YOU
COULD MANAGE this small job.

ps- could you give ME
my BALL BACK?

I, DOUGAL TRUMP, THINK IT'S VERY STRANGE

that my dad never hears me when I want to tell him something, goes deaf when I ask him for something, but the moment he hears the gentle tinkle of glass and the soft bounce of a football, his hearing goes on high alert and he automatically assumes that his innocent son has just kicked a football through the window.

I also find it very strange, and unfair, that his son (me) has got to clean the car for another eight weeks in order to pay for a new pane of glass. He doesn't understand that I was aiming for the top corner of my room and I missed.

Dads are very unfair.

But my dad won't be around much longer.

When he came storming into my room, with his eyebrows waggling all over the place and arms flapping, he went straight to the window to inspect the damage and found, among the broken glass, the key to the shed. I'd hidden it behind my ants' nest when it got too uncomfortable in my pocket. And now he's going to go to the shed to prove to everyone that I'm loopy.

He hasn't actually gone yet. Dad always takes ages to get around to doing things.

I, DOUGAL TRUMP, NOW KNOW what STAN AND BURT MEANT when they fluttered their hands up in the air. It was supposed to look like smoke rising. They were threatening to set fire to the shed!

Luckily Dad chose the right moment to finish the paper, check the football scores and go and prove that his son was loopy, by going to the bottom of the garden and opening up the shed.

That was when he saw Stan and Burt sneaking from our garden back into Stan's.

But they still tried to blame me. Stan said it was my idea to smoke the creature out of the shed so that everyone knew I wasn't loopy.

'Don't be ridiculous!' Dad shouted so loudly even I could hear. 'Ouch!' He was

stamping on the flames at the time. 'There is no creature in this shed! And just as soon as – ouch! – I've stamped these flames out – ow! – I will prove it!'

By now the flames had died down, leaving behind a great trail of smoke, which brought Mrs Grim hobbling out into the garden to rescue her washing, loudly complaining about thoughtless people who decide to burn their rubbish when their neighbours have their washing out.

'It's not rubbish, it's our shed!' yelled Dad.

Then he opened the door.

I don't know whether it was the smoke or the yelling that woke the creature up. It took one look at the crazy man coming through the door and leaped out of the hole at the back so fast that the shed finally

gave up trying to stand and collapsed in a heap all over Dad.

When Mrs Grim took her sheet off the washing line, she found the creature on the other side of it.

I don't know who was more frightened, Mrs Grim or the creature. Mrs Grim screamed, dropped the sheet and hobbled back indoors. The creature stood on its hind legs and beat its chest with its huge claws, baring its teeth and making a terrible noise.

From my vantage point at my bedroom window, I could see that the creature was big, black and hairy, with a white V on its chest, which reminded me of a jumper that Gran knitted for me when I was a child.

THE CREATURE!

I, DOUGAL TRUMP, AM ALIVE!!!

I, DOUGAL TRUMP, AM A HERO.

No one wants to kill me apart from Lysander Witzel and Sibble. Even Mrs Grim doesn't want to kill me, because she likes living next door to a hero – even if he did plant a furry mouse under her table.

Sibble wants to kill me because she's jealous of all the attention her heroic brother is getting.

Stan probably wants to kill me as well,

but that doesn't worry me because Burt won't let him.

This is what happened.

While Dad was trying to get bits of shed off himself, Stan tried to tell him that the fire was all my idea. Burt stood there listening. Then he told Stan to shut up.

Stan shut up. Dad stopped brushing himself down.

'It was Stan's idea to start the fire,' said Burt. 'And it was Stan's idea to dunk George in the river.'

'We'll talk about it later,' said Dad.

Typical. He always puts off the important jobs. But this time, I suppose he had a point. He was standing in Mrs Grim's garden with bits of shed all over him and a creature beating its claws against its chest. And Stan yelling over the fence that he was innocent.

I heard all this clearly because I was no longer in my bedroom. I was in Mrs Grim's garden by now, struggling to hold four arm plaster casts, one leg cast and one dog lampshade collar full of fruit. I went up to the creature, put it all down and offered it a banana that was poking out of the end of my arm cast Number Three. It stopped making its racket and took the banana. Then it sat down to enjoy the rest of the fruit that I shook out of my casts and the lampshade collar, while everyone gawped.

Then Mum came out to say that she'd telephoned the RSPCA and the police. Then Mrs Witzel came round to say she'd called the fire brigade and an ambulance. Then Mrs Grim came out to say she'd called the local council. She wanted them to know that it wasn't foxes digging holes in her garden and that we really should have wheelie bins.

Mrs Witzel said that if I'd harmed her son Stan by setting fire to him she'd—

Dad told her to shut up.

I asked if anyone had more fruit for the creature.

Everyone brought their fruit bowls round and the creature sat there happily eating while the police put a cordon round it so it couldn't escape until the RSPCA arrived. Then they had a word with Dad, after which they went off to have a word with Lysander Witzel.

But Lysander had scarpered.

Someone must have called the local newspaper, because they came round with their big cameras to take lots of photos of me. I ended up on the front page, with an article about how well I'd cared for the

creature and how I'd helped solve the mystery of the disappearing animals.

And it wasn't the creature eating the animals after all – it was Lysander Witzel!

I don't mean Lysander was eating the animals. He was stealing them.

Those boxes that he put in the gap between our houses were full of stolen small animals. They were all rare breeds of little furry creatures that are very hard to buy. The poor things were all drugged so they'd sleep quietly until Lysander sold them to people who were prepared to pay lots of money for them.

Lysander either stole the animals or got them from crooks who'd stolen them. Then he pretended to be a dealer in rare animals and sold them to innocent people for lots of money. He even sold a stolen

rabbit to Mum to give to Sibble.

Then he stole it back from Sibble and sold poor Bunnykins again. And I got the blame when it went missing.

What a crook.

He even stole Mrs Grim's cat, Precious.

Just before he moved next to us, someone stole a creature from London Zoo and left it in Lysander's shed. Only he got the wrong shed. He put the creature in our shed by mistake. Then he wrote a note for Lysander. But Lysander never got the note. I did.

And now I know what the creature was. Believe it or not, Claude was right when he said the creature was Baloo the bear from *The Jungle Book,* because that is exactly what Baloo is.

A giant sloth bear.

Giant sloth bears sleep during the day

and come out at night, when they forage for food, rattle trees hoping fruit will fall off, tear the bark looking for ants, dig holes and make grunting noises. My giant sloth bear was stolen from London Zoo, drugged and passed on to Lysander Witzel, along with a note – which I ate.

Lysander expected to find the creature in his shed when he moved in, but it wasn't there. That's why he was so interested in our shed – he thought the creature might be in it. He was supposed to keep it for a few days and then it would be collected by the person who was buying it – for a lot of money.

But the buyer never came for it. And Lysander thought the creature hadn't been stolen after all. He thought it had never arrived.

If the dog hadn't chased my football

down to the even wilder end of the garden that day, I don't know what would have happened to the creature. I'm sure Lysander wouldn't have cared for it like I did.

The creature is now back in London Zoo, where she has gone to join her husband and family. He was a she creature, not an it.

The London Zoological Association, who look after London Zoo, have given me life-time free membership, so I can go and look at my sloth bear as often as I like.

I, Dougal Trump, like being a hero.

I, DOUGAL TRUMP, AM FEELING VERY HAPPY.

Even though I've been forced to help Mum sort out my room before we take everything up to my new room in the loft, I'm still happy. I'm so happy, I even agreed to throw away a whole load of my stuff, including my mouldy conkers, my bag of stinky sand and my collection of plaster casts, which I admit were getting a bit smelly. Most of the other rubbish that came from the loft has gone into the skip – even though Dad insisted it was all worth a lot of money or might come in useful. Mum insisted.

Dad spends quite a lot of time rummaging through the skip these days.

I have several reasons to be happy.

First of all – the Witzels are moving!!

Lysander was eventually found by the police and is now somewhere answering their enquiries. The reason the Witzels moved here was because they wanted to go somewhere no one knew them, but now we know all about them, so they're off again.

Burt told Mr Truss everything. He said that Stan had tricked him as well. Stan said that if Burt helped tip George in the river, he'd make sure Lysander played him in goal all the time instead of me. Stan is a big fat liar like his dad.

Burt also tried to warn me that Stan wanted to smoke the creature out of the shed. That's why he tried to see me when I was grounded and why he made those fluttering movements with his arms that made him look silly.

I'm sorry to say that Burt isn't as

stupid as I thought. What I mean is, I'm sorry I thought he was stupid. Because he isn't. He's just a bit bigger than everyone else. Quite a lot bigger.

Another reason I'm feeling very happy is because I've been given a reward for all those pets that were stolen and have now been returned. Sibble now has her rabbit back, even though it was stolen. It's a rare Enderby Island rabbit. They are normally a smoky colour, so Sibble's creamy-coloured one is even rarer. He was given back to Sibble to say thank you for having a heroic brother who found the crook who'd stolen Bunnykins's mother and brothers and sisters.

Sibble still won't give me her rabbit, but I'm working on it.

But the best reason for feeling so

happy is because I am now star goalie for Fairford United. Tom asked me to join them after I was unfairly kicked out of Ocklesford Rovers, to play in goal instead of Billy. Billy's arm wasn't really broken, only sprained, but he now plays in midfield. If it wasn't for me, Tom would never have found out how good Billy is in midfield.

Burt Ironside has joined Fairford United as well. He plays in defence and is brilliant – the opposition are far too scared to get the ball past him.

Claude still plays for Fairford United and spends most of his games running around wondering what to do. But we don't mind, because Claude is Claude.

The old Fairford coach is coaching my old team, Ocklesford Rovers. Several ex-Fairford United players have gone over to play for Ocklesford Rovers. This was the score at our last match:

Fairford United 6 – Ocklesford Rovers 0

I didn't let in a single goal.

I, DOUGAL TRUMP,
AM A SUPERHERO.

Note to my stupid brother:
no you can't have my rabbit!
And if you say, 'I told you there was a creature in the shed,' one more time, I'm going to cover you in marmite and feed you to the dog.

NOTE TO the POLICE:
IF I HAVE BEEN ~~[illegible]~~ COVERED IN MARMITE AND FED TO the DOG, it WOULD HAVE BEEN SIBBLE.

How many times do I have to tell you my NAME is

SYBIL!

THIS IS THE LAST WILL AND TESTAMENT of me, Dougal Trump, of 13 Makepeace Avenue, Ocklesford, Middlesex. I, being of sound mind and body, make this will as follows:

My ashes must be scattered on the home ground of Fairford United Football Club, Fairford Road, Ocklesford, Middlesex. My ashes must be scattered by my best friends and teammates, George Quickley, Billy Truss, Burt Ironside and Claude Barleycorn.

I do not wish to be buried, because they would have to cut me in two and put half of me under each goal, from where I plan to make some spectacular saves.

To Tom, the coach of Fairford United, the best team in the world apart from Stamford United, I leave my new football boots. This is to—

DOUGIE,

PLEASE STOP WRITING WILLS AND COME OUT AND PLAY FOOTBALL!

OK, GEORGE, I'M COMING!

Leabharlanna Poibli Chathair Baile Átha Cliath
Dublin City Public Libraries

Acknowledgements:

I, Dougal Trump, would like to thank the writer Jackie Marchant, who was walking along our road when my mother finally achieved her greatest wish and threw a binbag of my stuff out of the window. The bag nearly landed on Jackie, then burst open to reveal everything that Mum had chucked out, including old notes from my friends and scribblings by me. Jackie Marchant took these bits of paper home and turned them into a book.

I would also like to thank Mike Lowery, for drawing the pictures.

I would also like to thank Alice Williams, for agreeing that my family are so weird that they had to go into a book.

I would also like to thank Emma Young and all 'Team Dougal' at Macmillan, for proving my innocence (despite all the charges levelled against me) by publishing this book. And for making this book look great.

Finally, I would like to thank all the kids who have written to me after reading this book – I am glad I am not alone in being blamed for everything.

And on that note, I love receiving your letters. But Mum is fed up with not being able to open the door because of all my fan mail, and Sibble is jealous because nobody ever writes to her.

So please could you send your letters to:

Dougal Trump
c/o Macmillan Children's Books
20 New Wharf Road
London N1 9RR

They will be kept in a neat pile for me to read in peace.

Thanks!

DOUGAL TRUMP

I'M
DOUGAL TRUMP...
Coming soon
WHERE'S MY TARANTULA?

The second hilarious book from the desk of Dougal Trump

Something truly horrible and terrible has happened. Something so awful that it is hard to put into words. But I will try.

Sybil has vanished!

(Not Sibble, my sister. If that happened, I wouldn't be upset at all.)

It is my beautiful eight-legged Goliath bird-eating spider Sybil who has disappeared. Perspex cage and all.

But if anyone can overcome this disaster it is I, Dougal Trump: superhero, local celebrity and brilliant goalkeeper for Fairford United.

DANNY BAKER
RECORD BREAKER

THE WORLD'S BIGGEST BOGEY

STEVE HARTLEY

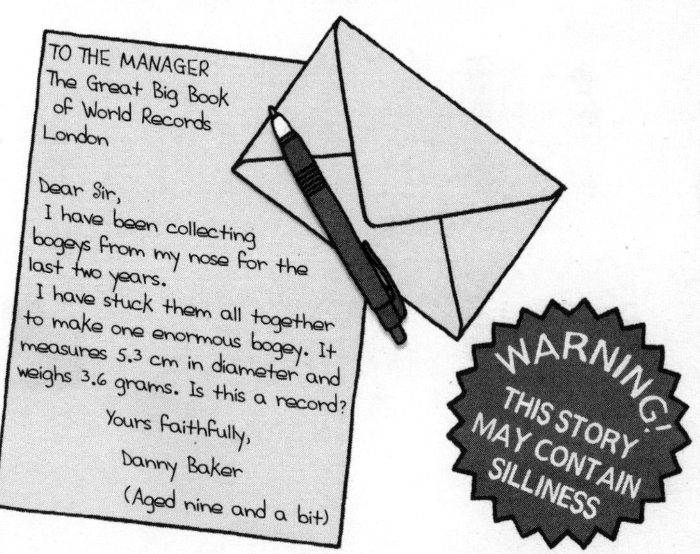
TO THE MANAGER
The Great Big Book
of World Records
London
Dear Sir,
I have been collecting bogeys from my nose for the last two years.
I have stuck them all together to make one enormous bogey. It measures 5.3 cm in diameter and weighs 3.6 grams. Is this a record?
Yours faithfully,
Danny Baker
(Aged nine and a bit)
WARNING!
THIS STORY MAY CONTAIN SILLINESS

Join Danny as he attempts to smash a load of revolting records, including:

LOUDEST TRUMP!
CHEESIEST FEET!
NITTIEST SCALP!

OUT NOW!

CHECK OUT THE DOUGAL TRUMP WEBSITE!

You'll find . . .

MORE FROM THE DESK OF DOUGAL TRUMP

BRILLIANT COMPETITIONS

Don't miss it!